THE BOUNTYMEN

Tom Quinlan headed a bunch of other bounty hunters to bring in the long-sought Dave Cull, who was not expected to be alone. That they would face difficulties was clear, but an added complication was the attitude of Quinlan's strong-minded woman, Belle. And suddenly, mixed up in the search for Cull, was the dangerous Arn Lazarus and his men. Hunters and hunted were soon embroiled in a deadly game whose outcome none could predict.

Books by Tom Anson
in the Linford Western Library:

A PLAGUE OF GUNFIGHTERS

TOM ANSON

THE
BOUNTYMEN

Complete and Unabridged

LINFORD
Leicester

First published in Great Britain in 1997 by
Robert Hale Limited
London

First Linford Edition
published 1999
by arrangement with
Robert Hale Limited
London

British Library CIP Data

Anson, Tom
The bountymen.—Large print ed.—
Linford western library
1. Western stories
2. Large type books
I. Title
823.9'14 [F]
ISBN 0–7089–5412–X

Ulvers

Published by
F. A. Thorpe (Publishing) Ltd.
Anstey, Leicestershire

Set by Words & Graphics Ltd.
Anstey, Leicestershire
Printed and bound in Great Britain by
T. J. International Ltd., Padstow, Cornwall

This book is printed on acid-free paper

1

Quinlan had been in no two minds about what to expect, and he had been right. It was not well received by Belle. There had been a letter that had been following Quinlan, from a man named Bishop, and now Quinlan was coming back from the telegraph office, having sent off a guarded but positive telegram in reply. Now with Belle, she in her midnight blue dress, he was in an upper hall of the Algonquin, approaching the room they had been occupying for the past two weeks. Two weeks, mainly because Belle had become tired of being so often on the move. Money was not of immediate concern. There was still an agreeable accumulation of bounty. This, now, was the core of Belle's straight-mouthed argument. A middle-sized, slim, but rounded woman with a mass of corn-coloured hair and dark eyes, she was also a woman who had never been short of an opinion. But they had stayed together, good times and bad, she and Quinlan, for some good while, Belle by no means inclined to stand in awe of him, who he was, his reputation. So she advanced her present opinion in spite of the big sum that was still on offer for Cull.

'You don't need it, Tom. Anyway, what about those others? How many? Two?'

'Three. Bishop, Naylor and Macafee. The money might be out for Cull, but the chances are he's not alone.'

'So, split *four* ways.'

'Even so, it's still one hell of a heap of money.'

'What *is* it about Cull? Apart from the money? There's something more.'

'He's sent some real good men to their Maker.'

'But he was last heard of, for certain, how long ago? Years. For years, nothing. And now here he is again. So another thing, Tom, is why?

Why would he suddenly take the sort of risks that has the whispers going already?'

Following her inside the room he went about turning lamps up, then hung his hat in a closet, 'There has to be some damn' good reason.'

Belle had taken her blue hat off, and her gloves and put them away, and now she stood before a wall-mirror touching at her hair. In the glass, too, she was looking at Quinlan. In his grey suit, shiny black boots, with his gold watch-chain, and though a tall, usually unsmiling man with coarse skin, thick black hair and black, hanging moustaches, his present style might almost have placed him, in the minds of most observers, as a well-off merchant. Still primping, Belle saw him take his scratched leather valise from the bottom of the closet, place it on one of the straight-backed chairs and open it. From it he took a carefully kept holster and a thickly shelled belt, brass shining dully, and these items he put on the bed. He then took out a stag-handled pistol, a Smith and Wesson Model Number 3, of blued steel, a .44 with an 8-inch barrel. It had been lovingly kept, and now Quinlan was giving it a thorough inspection, turning it over in his big hands, sighting it, spinning the cylinder. With great deliberation, he began loading it.

Belle turned away from the mirror. 'Where will they come to? Here?'

Such was his concentration that it was a few seconds before he glanced up quickly and answered her. 'Here? No. We don't want unnecessary words wafting out on the wind. There's a place a few miles out that they'll come to.'

'How soon?'

'Five days from now.'

'And you'll move out right after they come?'

'Yes, as soon as they arrive.'

'Well, you're not going to leave me here.' It was not a question.

'You could go back to Stoll River and wait there.'

'I could, but I sure won't. I'm coming part of the way with you. They can like it or lump it.' She might just as well have said, *and so can you*. She could see by the set of him that he did not like it at all and his dark gaze was fastened on her, perhaps probing for some evidence of irresolution. After all this time he must surely have known that he was seeking it in vain.

'Part of the way. How far?'

'You've not said where he is. Where you think he is.'

'Heading for country down on the Dead River. Something's drawing Cull into that area.'

'Maybe. But what? Tom, he could have a dozen men there.'

'Or a woman.'

'He's got women all over, so you've said. Or he did have.'

'I've no doubt he still has. A ladies' man, Cull.'

5

'*Cull Cull Cull*! God, Tom, I was sure we'd heard the last of that man's name long since.'

Quinlan could understand her disappointment. Earlier they had been talking of quitting this place and going up to Arizona, to Phoenix, where she had some kinfolk. Not having a fixed place, an accepted base, was the product of the way Quinlan's life had shaped itself. But even when there was no reason, he was a man who quickly became restless, forever wanting to be on the move. So now she came back to the question of Phoenix. 'We'll still be going there after Cull's done with?' Cull, *done with*, just like that. Belle knew better. Perhaps she had put it that way simply to needle him.

'That's what was agreed.'

'I expect that means yes.' The certain tension was present, the due recording of displeasure.

Quinlan had replaced pistol, holster and shellbelt in the much-travelled valise, which he had returned to the

6

closet. From that same place, however, he had fetched out a Winchester repeating rifle and now went through the same ritual of inspection and trial as earlier he had done with the pistol, quite absorbed, as though the woman was not even in the room. It was something which, in her present humour, she was not prepared to accept. The door-latch clicked. 'I'll be downstairs in the dining-room.'

★ ★ ★

In the dying light of the day, walking the roan horse to a stop among aspens, Dave Cull sat for several minutes, gloved hands clasped on the saddle horn, staring through the interstices of branches towards the homestead, its yard and various outbuildings. The once-orderly fields were neglected, overgrown, their borders now but faintly defined, lending to the scene a sense of desolation.

A man less cautious might have

walked the horse on, making a direct approach. Not Cull. Instead he turned about and began making a wide circuit at an ambling pace, keeping the homestead in view but examining all of the rolling country around it, and at the same time seeking any signs of the recent passage of other horses. It was near to a half hour before he satisfied himself that there was no company here and no evidence of any in preceding days, and came once more into the shelter of the aspens.

A long-legged, long-bodied man, sinewy, wearing black pants and shirt and a high-collared grey jacket, he also had on a shallow-crowned grey hat, much stained, leather thongs hanging either side of his face. A striking man, Cull, brown sideburns framing a visage that, stubble-whiskered though it was now, was unarguably handsome.

Miles away, beyond the homestead, hills whose folds only a little time ago had appeared blue were now but a misted, purple outline, and in the sky that was dark to the east while still holding faint light in the west, one or two stars were glimmering.

When Cull started the horse clear of the trees, heading directly towards the house, bit-chains clinking, this time his approach must surely be heard within. That was confirmed almost as soon as he began crossing the hardpack of the yard, with some kind of movement at the yard-door. Not raising his deep voice particularly, he called, 'Concepta . . . ?'

'Si . . . '

'It's me, Dave Cull.'

A rustling sound, of skirts, in the doorway.

'You come quick now, Señor Cull . . . !'

Innately cautious though, he asked, 'Anybody else been here?'

'No, Señor Cull . . . nobody. You come quick . . . !'

He swung down, walked forward and tied the roan to a hand-rail of the porch. Then he went up the three thick wooden steps onto the porch and in through the door. As soon as he got inside he thought that, even had he not known, he would have been able to smell the proximity of death.

2

At one time it had been a dwelling of some kind, with other, lesser buildings nearby, but these had vanished long ago, only a few pieces of greyed timber testament to their existence. The principal structure, too, was in an advanced state of decay, gaping holes in its roof, its doors hanging by rusting hinges, and windows devoid of glass. The place was empty of furniture, the bare wooden floors thick with grime. The best that could now be said of it was that it was possible — the three horses, one of them a pack animal, having been tied to what remained of a porch-rail — to step inside into comparative shade. The sun was by no means fierce, but Belle unfailingly took any opportunity to find a cooler place to be. This time she had said, *'It will be hot enough, on the journey.'* Tempted to observe that coming with him had been her decision alone, Quinlan had elected to say nothing.

What he did do — first testing the floorboards with a probing boot — was take up a position at a north-facing window-opening, and from time to time take out and consult his gold pocket-watch. Today Quinlan was dressed not in his townsman's suit but in a pair of narrow, dark-coloured worsted pants, a light grey shirt with a black string tie and a black vest; and on his head was a black, shallow-crowned hat. His boots, of a cowman's style, were not new, and plain and serviceable, but had no spurs attached to them. Neither was he wearing the Smith and Wesson pistol; but scabbarded on a sorrel horse outside, was the Winchester.

Belle had on a plain white cotton blouse and a divided skirt, ochre in colour, and a pair of light tan boots. Her hat was of felt, round of crown and wide-brimmed and her riding-gloves were of soft brown leather. At the present time she had peeled them off, occasionally slapping them lightly into the narrow palm of her left hand, an outward manifestation, perhaps, of gathering irritation.

Some of their belongings they had arranged to be stored at the Algonquin against their return, the items required for travelling being carried on a livery pack-animal hired by Quinlan, a placid, dun-coloured horse, but in Quinlan's opinion sound enough, and with a durable, dogged look about him. *'Good'n fer the long haul,'* the liveryman had said when Quinlan had told him that he intended riding west from there on a survey, for certain eastern interests, a story that Quinlan had thought worth floating. But this, now, was the agreed meeting-place. All they had to do was wait for the others. After a while Belle advanced the hope that they had got the day right. 'We could be here all night.'

'Then we'll make a camp.' She gave

up, then, knowing that he would have a sharp answer for any complaint she chose to make. She looked out through the twisted doorway. The horses were standing quietly, the pack-animal, Quinlan's sorrel and the bay that was now hers. Quinlan said, 'There's one coming.'

Belle crossed to where he was and looked out through the gap where once the window-pane had been. Indeed, one horseman leading a pack-animal and approaching unhurriedly, too far off yet to identify. But even at a distance — Quinlan waiting for the rider to close by another hundred yards — it becomes possible to recognize the way a known man sits the saddle, holds his body, his hands and his head, the certain attitude of him.

She sensed his recognition. 'Which one is it?'

'Kel Bishop.'

Watching the man and horses coming, the rider jouncing along, looking only to his front, after another half-minute,

14

she, too, could see that it was indeed Bishop.

Eighty yards short of the tumbledown structure, Bishop drew to a halt and hauled his packhorse in on a shorter lead. He sat studying the place, his horse wagging its head. From where he was he would not be able to see the tied horses. Quinlan turned, went on past Belle, her faint perfume coming to him, and walked outside and around the side of the place. As he came clearly into the horseman's view he raised one hand. Bishop kneed his horse, walking it on, towing the pack-animal. Before he reached Quinlan, Belle came out.

Bishop rode up, drew to a halt, and with some evidence of stiffness, dismounted. Surprisingly clean-shaven, as though he might have come out of a barber's, he was clad in Levis and a tan shirt, with a blue bandanna at his throat and he had a pistol hung about him, the holster tied down. He touched the brim of his black hat to Belle and did not even raise his eyebrows at her

15

presence. She knew that was Bishop's style, but knew, too, that numerous questions would be running through his mind. Quinlan found an exposed board that was still firm enough for the purpose, and helped Bishop tie his horses, before asking, 'How far are they?'

'An hour maybe.' From a saddlebag Bishop took a brass, telescoping spyglass and tapped gloved fingers on it. 'Had this on their dust a time back. They're in no hurry.' But they were coming. That was the important thing. Then Bishop did say, 'Didn't expect to find you here, Belle.'

'Then it's just as well there was no money riding on it,' she said, 'like there is on Dave Cull.'

Bishop's very dark blue eyes flicked to Quinlan and back again. If, as seemed likely, he wanted to ask how far Belle intended going, for it was plain that she was dressed for travel, he did not do so.

They all went inside the derelict

building. In a little less than an hour, Quinlan, nearest the window, nodded. Bishop's spyglass clicked as he opened it out, then lined it up. Silently, for perhaps a quarter of a minute, he studied oncoming riders and their horses. Then he said, 'Naylor an' Macafee. An' they're haulin' a pack-horse.' So, that would be another part of the little cavalcade that would soon ride on from here, a woman, four men and three pack-animals. Quinlan, Belle and Bishop walked outside.

As they neared those waiting at the derelict building, the incoming riders could be seen to be wearing identical long, buff-coloured dusters, and their tall-crowned hats were similar. The riders, however, were quite different in build and aspect. Naylor, a man in his late forties, had a long, hound's face, deeply creviced. He could easily have been taken for a disillusioned preacher. Macafee, on the other hand, was round-faced and ruddy, inclined to paunchiness, and was more than fifty years old.

When they had dismounted, and before Naylor had stepped back to check the security of all the gear on the pack-horse, both nodded to Belle and touched the brims of their hats. They remained unsmiling, however, and though asking no questions, had made it clear enough by their attitude that they would soon be looking for an explanation. Anything that seemed to cut across an enterprise that was to be conducted by professionals would need explaining.

There followed a brief discussion on the direction that would be taken from this point on, and about the last word that anybody had heard concerning Cull.

'It's not changed, then,' Bishop said. 'As far as we can tell, it's still the Dead River country.'

'Yeah, an' that's a good long haul,' Macafee said, but he was looking past Bishop, at Belle, 'so we'll want to get a

18

move on.' Once before, long ago, Cull had eluded them. Clearly, Macafee was anxious that the still-rankling failure be put to rights. He was touching a whitish scar on his right wrist, perhaps linking it to its origin.

Taking the initiative, Quinlan said, 'Belle's coming part of the way.' Now he looked at her. 'It's my opinion you'd be best to wait in Dolomite.'

Briefly Belle closed her eyes as though summoning up pictures of the terrain and specific places to come. When she opened them she said, 'Dolomite. There's another town though, isn't there, between there and the Dead River?'

'Abbott's Forge,' said Bishop who, before he had set out, had been looking at maps. 'But I reckon you'd be a whole lot more comfortable in a place like Dolomite.'

Absorbing that, she then asked, 'Couldn't he be anywhere along the Dead River?'

'He could,' Bishop conceded, 'but that area, out beyond Abbott's Forge, that seems to be the likeliest place to start.' Whether he actually knew something or was merely opting for the most directly approached place along that river, as a starting-point, could not be adduced from his tone or his expression. Quinlan did not add anything to this small discussion but what Bishop had been saying was in line with his own thoughts. It was Naylor who said, 'We'll sure find Cull. We'll get it done this time.' They glanced at Naylor with his old-dog's face, and perhaps their minds went back to the shoot in wind-torn dust at a place far from here, known as Culpepper's Camp, all four men who were here now, and three others: Gully, Sansom, Troup. They had been convinced that they had got Dave Cull cornered, even when it was conceded that he had some hard men with him, men who had nothing more to lose, perhaps as many as seven of them, though it had been next to impossible to tell, in the very bad conditions.

★ ★ ★

Quinlan had got as far as the overturned
wagon, his canteen-soaked bandanna
tied over nose and mouth, lying half
rolled on one side, gripping his rifle,
almost praying for the bowling yellow
dust to clear, hearing sounds of fierce
shooting across to his right.

Sansom, who he had come seeking,
should have been around here somewhere, but he had not responded to
recent calling. Quinlan almost hugged
himself into the ground as lead came
hammering into the wreck of the
wagon, but whether it meant he
had been seen or that somebody was
merely traversing the area on the fly, it
was impossible to tell. It was resolved
when another bullet came whanging
in, this one whining away off some
metal part of the wagon. On boots,
knees and elbows, hat-brim flattening
against the side of his face, in the
wind, Quinlan began moving again.
One problem though, was that if he

21

were to get too far out in front he would be at serious risk of stopping one from somebody in his own party.

It was then that he came upon the dust-mantled body of Sansom, the top of his head missing, and what remained, moving with green-backed flies. An as-yet unknowing widow three hundred miles away.

They were shooting at the wagon again. That told Quinlan that his change of position had not been seen. Still the thick dust was blowing. He could hear horses whickering and thought he could also hear voices calling. Then he caught sight of a man in a red shirt, a man he had glimpsed earlier. Now, that was definitely one of Cull's. Name unknown. But here, with Cull, which was all that mattered. Now, though, there was only the moving dust again. Or was there? No. There. The red shirt. Quinlan shot fast and knew that he had hit him.

Quinlan, his eyes smarting, began edging backwards, but when he had covered a matter of only three or four yards, during a momentary thinning of dust he distinctly saw Cull, but by the time he got the rifle lined up the man he most wanted was gone. Quinlan cursed and continued his awkward, backwards movement and he had covered maybe twenty yards in that fashion when he heard Bishop call to him, and presently Bishop himself, on hands and knees, came alongside him.

'Sam Gully's caught one.'

'Bad?'

'Yeah.' With a gloved hand Bishop gestured at his own throat. 'He ain't about to go anywhere.'

Quinlan nodded. 'I hit the one in the red shirt. And Cull's still here. I've seen him.'

'This is a shit of a place,' Bishop said. 'We go forward, they'll pick us off. We go back an' we lose the best chance at the bastard we're ever gonna get.'

Nearby, someone was on the move.

23

Augie Troup, dust plastered all over the sweat on his face, said, 'Gully's done fer.'

'Jesus.' Bishop was struggling to check the remaining loads in his pistol, a Colt.

Quinlan asked Troup, 'Where's Macafee?' Troup, blinking because his eyes were smarting, merely moved his head. 'He don't look pleased.' Little wonder. A bullet had broken his right wrist and he would be in a lot of pain, and God alone knew how long this inconclusive fight was going to go on. Conditions could scarcely have been worse.

About then, they began pulling back, their heads ducked down and away because of the driving dust, until they got across to the hurt Macafee, sitting holding his bloodied wrist with his left hand, his face drawn, and suddenly very old-looking. Six or seven yards away, Naylor lay with his dead horse, rifle in hand, doing his best to sight anything he could shoot at.

"There's only one way the bastards can come,' Naylor said, 'an' that's this way.' Certainly, that was the case, high, clay-faced cliffs rising behind where Cull and the others were, Quinlan's bountymen blocking the way out. Bishop shouted, 'Horses comin' . . . !'

Sure enough, but only one. And there it was, across to their left, a brownish, urgently moving shape, there and then gone, riderless, terrified by something, or maybe crazed by the stinging dust. One of Cull's.

Naylor had got to his feet, eyes slitted above the red bandanna tied over his nose. 'We'd best not stay bunched up.' Some reckoned to have this sixth sense whenever things got bad, and Naylor happened to be one of them. Whether it was because of this or not, he was giving good advice. Leaving the gasping Macafee where he was, Quinlan, Bishop, Naylor and Troup put some distance between themselves; and none too soon. Possibly the lone, hard-running horse was being got ready for a rush by Cull and his men and had broken away, for suddenly, out of the tearing yellow clouds came the shapes of mounted men, men who were shooting as they rode.

Quinlan, down on one knee, shot, levered and shot again. Bishop fired and a horse went down, hurling its rider forward over its neck, and when, surprisingly quickly, the man came to his feet, Naylor shot him. A horse that was double-mounted loomed close, and Troup, Quinlan and Bishop all shot at a target that, at the range, could scarcely be missed. Both men went down, bouncing and rolling, arms and legs flailing, and the horse went charging on, reins flying loose.

But Cull. Where the hell was Cull? Lead was whipping in. Abruptly Troup sat down, losing his rifle. Bishop tracked a quirt-lashing rider and whacked him, but the man stayed in the saddle, jouncing slackly as he was carried away out of their vision. Quinlan and Naylor shot again, and a man in what looked like a blue shirt rose in his stirrups, then slowly sagged down and fell off the lunging horse. Quinlan crawled to where Troup had now fallen over, and when he came back, squinted across at Bishop and shook his head.

After that, there was only the wind and the dust. No more horsemen. Quinlan saw no profit in blundering around in these very bad conditions. If any of those they had brought down were still living, a man could walk into a bullet and never see the shooter.

Quinlan called, 'We'll wait. Stay put.' He could not know that the wind would not slacken, then die away, for another three hours.

So they went back and hunkered down near Macafee, who was now barely conscious. Macafee wounded, Gully, Sansom and Troup all dead. It did not seem possible. All good men.

When the dust had all but gone there was laid bare the desolation all around them. It must have been like waking up on a battlefield. Dead men and dead horses seemed to be everywhere, all filmed over with dust. Forty yards from where they had waited lay the body of the man who had not immediately fallen from the saddle. Quinlan and Bishop went around looking one by one at those who had been brought down, dwarfed by the rearing, clay-faced cliffs, a place that seemed to be on the very edge of nowhere, just the dead men and animals, a wrecked wagon, some bedrolls, canteens, pistols, rifles, a coffee pot. But there was no sign of Dave Cull. He was not among the dead. Bishop, for one, was reluctant to accept that Cull had got by them, even with the dust blowing the way it had been. Quinlan thought that maybe the devil did look after his own. What he said was, 'We'll need to see to the burials.' All of them. Troup, Gully and Sansom as well. There was no way they were going to pack them out all that distance, no matter what the widows might have to say about it, later.

★ ★ ★

Quinlan led off, trailing a pack-horse, then came Belle, then Bishop and his pack-horse, then Naylor with Macafee and their pack-animal. Before leaving, looking to the horses and the security of the loads, they had exchanged a few words about Cull and it had become clear to Belle, so she thought, that this was a small group that was joined by a very firm purpose. For the first time she felt a true sense of division, of being set apart from Quinlan, of becoming a person of the second rank. It had been a feeling that had strengthened as soon as the entire group had come together and had fallen into an old, easy familiarity, the product of having passed together through testing times. Mounting, near to Quinlan but happen-stance a little distance away from the others, in a lowered voice she had said, 'I know quite well now what it's all about. I should have picked it long since. It's not about the money at all, or about the dead men. It's about pride. You — none of you — could swallow what Cull did to you, making you look like fools.'

Quinlan had almost rounded on her but with an effort had turned away, saying brusquely, 'Mount up.' The displeasure had been in his tone, though, and the eyes of Bishop and Macafee and Naylor had met briefly. Naylor's face, as he had swung up, staring at the woman's narrow back, had plainly displayed what had been going through his mind. *'This is a bad start. A bad omen.'* A man always ready to consider omens, Naylor.

3

Hatless, Cull was in the deeply shadowed room where the woman lay slipping towards death. Near the bed a single lamp was glowing, illuminating a half-moon table with numerous small, coloured bottles cluttered on it. A brown one he picked up, uncorked it and sniffed cautiously. Laudanum. He recorked it. Half turning, he motioned the Mexican woman into the room.

'The doc, he's been here?'

'Si . . . Come three, four time . . . No more can do. Come here no more.'

'He tell yuh that?'

'Si.'

Cull studied her for a moment or two, then nodded. The woman took it as dismissal and withdrew but she could still be seen, waiting in the hallway. The sick-room was a stuffy place, full of strange odours, a place kept airless too long.

The woman lying in the narrow cot had had the bedclothes pulled up as far as her throat and was quite still, her dark head resting on a single pillow, her gaunt face slick with sweat. So shallow was her breathing now, that there was scarcely any perceivable movement; but now, for the second time since he had come into the room, her eyelids flickered and he bent close, his long shadow thrown across cot and wall.

From the hallway Concepta could hear only the murmuring of the man's voice, not what was said, but now he turned his head to look in her direction. 'Now's the time.' Genuflecting, the old Mexican woman went scuffing as quickly as she could along the hall.

★ ★ ★

False-fronts stood cut sharply against the night sky. Somewhere, somebody was strumming a guitar. Tied horses were stamping and from time to time, whickered. A few lamps were glowing. Sometimes, sounding flatly on the windless air, there was a sudden rush of laughter.

In a back-room in a saloon known as Cody's, men were sitting in on a desultory card-game, faces half in shadow, other men lounging, watching, others coming and going. All of a sort, those in here, left to their own devices and best left alone. These were the hours and this was the kind of place where word often came in, brought sometimes in the first instance by drifting, dusty horsemen, by whiplashing teamsters, railroaders or drummers, where a man got to hear of certain things simply by sitting listening.

Asa Lodd came in. Jack Guido and Joshua Phelps were among those sitting at the table, all of them raggy, hard-eyed, unwashed men, men to step well clear of. Lodd bent close behind Guido's head.

'Where's Arn?'

'Upstairs.'

'Got to have me a word.'

Guido said, 'He'll not thank yuh fer walkin' in, not 'til he's got done with the whore.'

Lodd straightened up. Plainly he was uncertain but still anxious.

Looking up from his cards, Phelps said, 'Fer Chrissake Asa, sit down. Yuh look like yuh jes' shit yore ownself.'

'An' if yuh go pull Arn off'n that yeller whore afore he's done, that's sure on the cards,' said Guido.

'Arn'll want to know what it is I heeard,' Lodd said.

'Then git on up an' wait in the hall,' Phelps suggested.

'What room's he in?'

'The one where yuh kin hear the whore yellin'.'

For a few seconds Lodd stood looking at Phelps, then left.

If Lodd and the two card players were men to avoid, ugly men with dead eyes, Arn Lazarus was one to put the fear of God into all but the foolhardy. A man nearing fifty, lean, with a prominently boned face, a face copiously and deeply lined, dark stubble flecking his long jaw, his skin coarse and pitted, his often partly exposed teeth were broken and yellowed and, set in deep sockets, his eyes were strangely pale, almost colourless, the left one partially closed, the lid scarred, having been damaged at some time. His clothing was greasy and he stank.

The appearance of Lazarus when he came in with Lodd caused some who were there to find reason to leave rather than stay and perhaps draw his attention. The few who remained, other than Guido and Phelps were given short shrift by Lazarus and departed at once, leaving behind them only a mist of tobacco smoke and a couple of abandoned poker hands. Lodd shut the door. Lazarus did not sit down. Instead, giving every evidence of being unsettled, he was moving around the room and making odd, shrugging movements with his shoulders, sometimes lifting and resettling a shellbelt that was heavily, brassily loaded, an old-model Colt pistol with a rakish handle jutting from a well-used holster. In this mood, Lazarus made even men such as these fall quiet. Nobody, no matter how well acquainted with him, could ever be sure which way he might jump, or when. Terrifyingly dangerous. One careless word could tip the balance. Of Lodd he now demanded, 'Where'd yuh hear it?'

'Freighters. Fellers that come in with wagons.'

'Come from where?' Lazarus was still moving restlessly, apparently without purpose.

'Morkell. 'Round there.' Blinking, looking at Lazarus, Lodd said then, 'Some word says he's headin' on down to the Dead River country.'

Lazarus stopped moving, stood quite still.

Cull's face has become two, then

36

merges into one again. In the hot,
stinking cabin there are three of them,
him, Cull and Josie, bottles on the table
and rolling around the floor. There is
no laughter now. It has gone sour and
turned to acrimony, the woman's voice
stridently riding over the voices of the
men. 'Yuh ain't no ways good enough
to take Arn, Dave! Yuh never was an'
yuh never will be!' Cull, infuriated, is
pushing at Josie, yelling for her to shut
her mouth, while Lazarus, unsteady,
drunker than Cull, is flailing at him,
then suddenly finds himself on the
slippery floor, his lower lip cut.

It was better not to say anything
to Lazarus when he fell into one of
these strange, angry silences. Anyway
he would scarcely be aware of being in
this room. He would be in some other
place, in the past, and in some way
to do with Dave Cull and a woman.
Lazarus's woman, Josie-something. A
long way back. But by God, it had never
gone away. Somebody now opened the
door and looked in but at Guido's

abrupt motion, withdrew and closed the door. Lazarus did not seem to have noticed.

He is on hands and knees on the liquor-sticky boards, his head hanging, his senses spinning;. He thinks he must have been hit very hard. He can hear Josie's voice and she is still cursing Cull, goading him. 'Where's your Goddamn' woman got to, Dave? Throwed yuh out?' Cull seems to have got real mad and he is shouting at her still, but he, Lazarus, hurt, saliva hanging from his mouth, can do nothing, partly stunned by a savage blow, his belly awash with bad whiskey, the edges of everything frayed. But he is doing his utmost to get back on his feet and get at the bastard. Josie is still screaming abuse, out of all control.

Phelps reached for a bottle and filled a shot-glass. When, without saying a word, he proffered it to Lazarus, the ugly man took it almost absently. Then Lazarus stared at the glass in his hand, swallowed the drink in one go and dropped the glass, which did not break but went rolling across the floor. Neither Guido nor Lodd had moved.

He is trying to rise. He can still hear the woman's voice and now it seems she is calling on all the dark demons of her beliefs to arise and destroy Cull. Now he, Lazarus, is on hands and knees again, the woman yelling, 'Kill him, Art . . . ! Kill the bastard . . . !' Then Cull's swinging boot comes crunching into his face, into the left eye, bloodying it, and the room goes spinning away again. So Lazarus does not see the woman find the pistol, does not see her, awkwardly, two-handed, trying to get it cocked, is not aware of Cull, in white fury, going to her with his knife, can but vaguely hear her shrieking in a different way as the blade goes in fast, once, twice, three times. Into woman and child.

'Bastard . . . !' Phelps stepped a half pace back. The entire place, not just this room, seemed to have fallen quiet. Maybe word had spread that it would be healthier to stay well clear of where Arn Lazarus was. Lazarus, coming to himself, reached and seized the bottle from Phelps and tipped it at his whiskery mouth, some of the fierce spirit coursing down his chin. Then he stood breathing hard, sweat starting on his forehead, trying to get his thinking straight. Maybe, at last, this was a real chance. Over a long time he had got word on the wind about Dave Cull, but not once had it come to anything. Yet Lazarus had put out his own word in various parts of the country. He had been convinced that there would come a day when he would come up with Cull. And not only Cull. There was a certain woman, so Lazarus had heard, a particular woman among a number, that Cull was closest to. Well, she would come to the same end as that other, Lazarus's own woman had, in the stinking cabin after a night of drinking. His pale eyes fastened on Phelps.

'I'll split the bitch with a blade, like

he done. An' him. By God I will, an' any brood there is.'

So they all knew well enough who it was he was talking about, and this time it might come to pass. Phelps certainly had a strong feeling about this latest word that had come in. The much-wanted Dave Cull, gone to ground and not heard of for a hell of a long time, suddenly being talked of again. If he had not been seen, why would his name come up? There were those, of course, who believed that the man was dead, indeed there were some who claimed to *know* it. Lazarus had never believed Cull dead. 'When he is, we'll *all* know it.' He tipped the bottle to his mouth again. Though he could not have known it, he now wondered aloud what others had wondered. 'But why would the bastard come out from wherever he was at?' Nobody had a ready answer, if, indeed, Lazarus expected one. But if Cull *was* out, then there had to be a powerful reason. He was wanted in too many places for it to be otherwise. And with every step he took, he must be aware that, no matter how much time had gone by, there had been wounds caused that would never heal, and that, given one whiff of his name, Lazarus, for one, would be bound to come for him.

Now Lazarus set the bottle down on the table among the tobacco ash and the stained playing cards. He said, 'If the word was the Dead River country, that's where we're headed.'

Guido ventured, 'An' if'n he's gone when we git there?'

'Then we'll track the bastard clear to Hell if we have to. An we'll take care of any kin o' his that we come across.' Cull, and everyone connected with Cull. Some of the strange fire that had been burning in Lazarus's pale eyes had died down but he was still unsafe and they knew it. Cull's very name seemed to drive this man to the very borders of madness. To Phelps, he said, 'Go git that mount o' yourn shoed. We don't want no delays nowhere, once we're on the move.' Phelps went out. To Guido and Lodd, Lazarus said, 'We'll want grub an' extra canteens. Do it now. Soon as Phelps walks that animal out o' the smith's, we'll be gone from here.' And one more town glad to see the back of them, for sure. That there were places they would pass through on the journey, where the law had a particular interest in Arn Lazarus and each of the men with him, seemed now to be considered of no account. They would deal with whatever came their way when it became necessary to deal with it, and by God, it would be a lawman careless of his own life who stood in the way of these four now that Lazarus had got a fresh sniff of Dave Cull.

★ ★ ★

They were not far along the trail, but Naylor and Macafee had fallen slightly further behind and so could exchange some views without being overheard. It was Naylor, in the main, who was unsettled and had been from the moment that he had seen Belle come out of that derelict place back there, to join Quinlan and Bishop. Dressed for riding.

Macafee asked, 'What's Bish think?'

Naylor tugged at the brim of his old hat and shrugged. 'Dunno. Can't tell. Bish was allers kinda tight with Quinlan. No word out o' place. No, she kinda gets under my saddle like a Goddamn' burr, Mac. Allers did.'

'She'll go only as far as Dolomite.'

'It's still a helluva long ride to Dolomite. I reckon it's gonna seem a whole lot longer.'

Macafee half turned in the saddle and gave a tweak on the lead to their pack-horse. 'Bastard's near asleep.' Then, 'If you'd known she'd be along, would you have come?'

Naylor dug in his shirt pocket for his sack of Bull Durham, and as he rode, built himself a smoke. Now he stared first to their left, then in the opposite direction, then screwed his body around and studied their back-trail. Macafee asked him what was up.

Naylor scraped a vesta on his rump and lit the skinny quirly he had fashioned, sweet blue smoke trailing. 'Got a real bad feelin', Mac.'

'What? Because of Belle?'

'Could be. Somethin'.' Naylor took another longer look behind them. Bishop must also have looked back and seen him doing it and called, 'What's up?'

Naylor turned to face ahead, shrugging. 'Nothin' Bish.' That was the trouble. Naylor had a distinct feeling that there ought to have been something. Bishop went on looking at him for a few more seconds, then turned to face ahead. Though Quinlan must have heard the exchange, he did not turn to look.

4

A night-camp with the fire flickering, the smell of hot bacon still in the air. The night was quiet, and down a shallow bank that was sparsely clumped with green brush, the narrow creek could be heard running over stones.

It had been a steady but determined leg of the journey that they had ridden, and in view of the fact that they had three pack-animals along, Quinlan was not displeased with the distance covered. Less pleasing was the reflection that there had been one or two straight-mouthed exchanges between himself and Belle. In the finish he had chosen to detach himself, riding on a further short distance ahead, an act not overlooked by Naylor and Macafee, nor, no doubt, by Bishop.

In the firelight, faces cast in shadow by broad hat-brims, the question of

46

Cull's movements and whereabouts surfaced again. It was Bishop who put forward a plan whereby a substantial length of the Dead River, on the stretch beyond Abbott's Forge, could be scoured for any signs of recent comings and goings, tracks in or out of the water, dead camp-sites, anything of interest.

'We can spread out,' Bishop said, 'take a day, coupla days to look, then come all together.'

It sounded like a reasonable approach, though Macafee, who now lay with his head propped against his saddle, his hat tipped over his face, said, 'What's between where we're at now, an' Dolomite?'

'There's no town,' Naylor said.

Quinlan said, 'There's a trading post this side of Warrior Bluff.' This, a land-feature in a stretch of undulating country, the highest points of which were some loaf-shaped hummocks too paltry to be called hills. 'Geddes's. It draws talk from up an' down the country like old meat draws flies.'

'No doubt we'll soon enough get to be part of the talk,' Macafee remarked, 'if we go there.'

'It's a kind of trade,' said Quinlan. 'Risking word going on ahead of us, against anything of value we might pick up there.' Naylor had been staring across the fire at the profile of the woman, but quickly averted his eyes when she turned her head. Suspended over the fire was a black wreck-pan with a handle on either side, water steaming in it. Belle stood up. Quinlan, anticipating her, also stood. 'I'll get it.' He took up two thick cloths that had been laid by and, as the woman collected up the tinware of their recent meal, used these to seize the handles of the wreck-pan and carried it down to the creek, Belle following with the utensils, a small, stiff-bristled brush with a handle, and a drying cloth. At the creek's edge she dumped her burdens into the wreck-pan and set about cleaning them with the brush, then drying them. The men had not budged from the fire, some sixty feet away. Quietly she said, 'They resent me.'

'They've said nothing. Nothing that I've heard, anyway.'

'They don't have to say anything. I can feel it. I'm not stupid.'

He had known that this outright declaration was coming but was oddly unprepared to argue against it. 'It's just that they're sure not used to having a woman along. It makes them feel uncomfortable.'

'What about? Sleeping near me? Having to give me a woman's privacy? Having to go tramping off somewhere to empty their own bladders?'

'No. It's the . . . responsibility. This is bad country. The further you go the worse it gets. It's not always the way it looks.'

'I've lived in the territories long enough to know that. They know it.'

'Belle, you should let it lie.'

She wanted to get it all off her chest,

though. 'Naylor looks like he could slit my throat.'

'You know by now what Naylor's like.'

'I thought I did. There's that, and there's the other thing.'

'What?'

She picked a platter out of the steaming water and hot-handed it, drying it and setting it aside. 'He's jumpy about something.'

'He gets these notions.'

'There he goes now.'

Quinlan looked. Naylor had stood up and had taken his rifle and was trudging away into shadows on the farther side of the camp. 'Naylor's a naturally cautious man. At a camp he likes to take a good look around, after dark. He's always done it.'

'Yes, well he makes me nervous, and he's always done that.' The last coffee-mug was dried.

Quinlan picked up the wreck-pan and poured its still-steamy water into the creek. He took the cloth from

Belle and wiped the interior dry. Belle stacked all the dried plates, mugs, forks and knives in it and Quinlan picked up the pan.

'We'll have to try to keep everything the way it is, 'til Dolomite.'

'Where I get dumped.'

'You wanted to come.'

She ignored it. 'How long do you reckon I'll finish up waiting around in Dolomite?'

'I can't even guess that. But look . . . Belle . . . Dave Cull's a real dangerous man. He could be alone or he could have men with him. Either way, you wouldn't want to be anywhere near him. An' I wouldn't want you to be.'

About to say *I can look out for myself*, she realized how absurd that was, and would serve to draw nothing but anger from Quinlan. She followed him as he carried the wreck-pan back to the fire. Bishop was in the act of throwing more sticks on, causing whirling sparks to go climbing away.

Macafee seemed to be asleep. Presently Naylor came pacing back out of the dark.

'All quiet?' Bishop asked.

Naylor mumbled something and laid the rifle down near where he intended sleeping. Bishop glanced at Quinlan and raised an eyebrow. Quinlan did not say anything.

Though there was no visible moon, some of the cloud that had been overhead had dissipated and a few icy stars were winking. Macafee was snoring. Belle dragged her saddle a few yards away and got her bedroll and spread it. Quinlan felt that she was not only putting distance between herself and the others but was sending a message to him at the same time.

★ ★ ★

By close to mid-day they came within sight of Geddes's Trading Post, the loaf-like mounds beyond it, and on the near-end of one, the whitish cut-off that, for reasons that were lost in time, was known as Warrior Bluff.

Bishop had been leading, towing his packhorse, but now reined in and waited for them all to close up behind him. 'Horses there.'

That was true. A couple of them hitched to a tie-rail out front. As the little cavalcade drew nearer to the sprawling, split-log and fieldstone building with its overhanging roof supported all around by poles, they could see that the horses did not look up to much, poorly kept and with very rough-looking gear on them. The approach was made slowly, and Quinlan said, 'I'd expect Dave Cull to have better horseflesh than that, but we can't take chances. When we get to about thirty yards out, all stop. Me an' Bish, we'll go on in an' take a look.' There was no discussion. Thirty yards or so short of Geddes's, Bishop tossed the lead of his packhorse to Belle, so she had charge of two pack-animals now, and he and Quinlan rode on. Macafee and Naylor slid their Winchesters free of their scabbards and, stocks resting on knees, sat their saddles watching and waiting.

At the trading post Quinlan and Bishop dismounted and tied their horses. They went in.

The interior was gloomy, for there were few windows and the place was cluttered with merchandise of all kinds. The smell in here was strong but unspecific, an amalgam of smells, from paraffin to animal hides and right now, the smell of unwashed humanity.

As well as the hang-bellied Geddes in his sweat-stained pink undershirt, there were two whiskery men in very old clothing, hunters, maybe, and not much luck in some while. Red-rimmed, watery eyes swung to examine Quinlan and Bishop. What they saw was sufficient to cause them concern for they straightened up from leaning attitudes at the counter, and stepped away. Geddes's pouchy eyes had all but disappeared. These men he thought he should know, but it was a few seconds before it came to him. When it did, he mentioned no names but merely nodded uncertainly.

Quinlan began examining some Indian blankets that were hanging from a stretched cord, while Bishop went outside to wave the others in. Presently their arrival could be heard, horses blowing, metal clinking. Then the door opened and Bishop came back in followed by Naylor and Macafee who no longer had rifles in hand. Then Belle came in and had not taken two paces before her nose wrinkled at the enclosed stench.

One of the greasy-looking, ragged men wandered away down among the stock, picking things up, putting them down. The other nodding to Geddes, went shuffling past the Quinlan party and on outside. One less to stink the place out.

Quinlan fronted the counter that Geddes was standing behind, and Bishop stood at his shoulder. 'You know who I am, an' you know Mr Bishop.'

'Yeah, sure do.' He might have extended a fat hand but neither of the men in front of him moved a muscle, so the impulse died.

'An' you'd know Dave Cull if he walked in.'

'Dave Cull?' The pig-eyes shifted from Quinlan to Bishop and back again. In his husky voice he said again, 'Dave Cull? Ain't nobody clapped eyes on Dave in Gawd knows how long.'

'Take your time thinking about it,' Quinlan said. 'If I get to know Dave's been here an' you've not said, I'll be back. Rely on it.'

'I swear to Gawd, Mr Quinlan, I ain't seen a whisker o' Dave Cull in years.'

'But you've got ears hangin' up among all this shit in here, Geddes. You get to hear things. Tell us about Cull. What you've heard.'

Geddes was sweating. 'A man hears all sorts all the time. Most of it is shit.'

'Cull. What have you heard about Cull?'

Geddes swallowed hard. 'He's on the move ag'in.'

'North, east, west, south?' Bishop was the snake staring dead-eyed at the jackrabbit.

'South. It was south that was said.'

The second of the ragged men, his eyes cast down, went easing on out. The door closed behind him. Naylor turned his dog's face in that direction, then he, too, went outside. Almost at once there came a shout and the sounds of a scuffle. Macafee was first out, then Quinlan, then Bishop, Belle following, but only as far as the doorway.

It was clear what had happened. The man who had first stepped outside had been at the packhorses, no doubt looking for any items worth stealing, but Naylor, ever suspicious, had caught him in the act, following the second man outside. Now Naylor was locked in a fierce struggle with the one at the horses, while Macafee got a-hold of the other. As Naylor got his man swung around, they came in staggering steps towards the building. Quinlan drew the Smith and Wesson and in a blue-glinting arc, swept it down to crack with devastating force against the hat of Naylor's adversary, a blow that felled the man. Naylor stood hands on hips, breathing deeply, his own hat fallen off during the struggle. Macafee released his man and in one stride, Quinlan was there, the barrel of the pistol shoved up under the man's jaw, tilting his bearded head back. His eyes were wide and seemed to be protruding. He was near to death and knew it.

But Quinlan took the pistol away and slid it back in its holster. He said, 'Get that load of shit there back on his horse an' get gone. Don't even look back. Move north an' keep moving north.' The man on the ground was rolling back and forth, moaning, his boots scraping as though seeking purchase, but to no avail. It took some four or five minutes to get him up and in his saddle, a man who, once there, was swaying uncertainly, his bushy face tilted to one side, blood on it, gasping noises coming from him. His companion was compelled to ride close alongside him, one arm fully extended, offering him some kind of support, and in that fashion the pair of them departed from the trading post, not looking back, all of Quinlan's party watching them, and Geddes, whose wide face was drained of all colour. He must have been taken aback when Quinlan turned on him and began questioning him again.

'What else is there, about Cull?' It was as though the incident with the drifters had never taken place.

'Nothin' else, Mr Quinlan.'

'There's something,' Quinlan insisted. He knew Geddes of old. If Geddes had thought that there was a chance that Quinlan would eventually come to accept that nothing further had been heard, he now realized that there was no chance at all of that.

'Nothin' about Cull.'

'What else, then? You've heard something else. What?'

Geddes's tongue flicked at his dry lips. 'Mr Quinlan, I dunno how good it is . . .'

'Tell me. You've got no more time left.'

Geddes said, 'There's some word come that there's others out, lookin' fer Dave Cull.'

'What others? Bountymen?'

'No.' Geddes seemed to be having some trouble getting the rest of it out. 'Arn Lazarus.'

All of them stood stock still, staring at Geddes. Finally, Quinlan asked, 'When did you hear this?'

'Few days back. It was kinda . . . wa-al, not certain. Come from a feller come in tryin' to sell some stuff. Claimed he heeard it in Pindar, real recent.'

Naylor's hound-face was thrust slightly forward, as though on a scent. Maybe the vague demons that seemed always to inhabit his back-trail had now taken on a fearsome, recognizable shape, and

60

Naylor had no liking at all for what he was seeing. It was he who repeated the name that Geddes had given. 'Lazarus.'

Macafee would need no elaboration, nor would Bishop, nor Quinlan. When Geddes had been curtly dismissed, thankful that he had got away without physical harm, it was only Belle for whom the name Lazarus needed some explanation, at least in connection with Dave Cull. When they were once again on the move, Quinlan told her.

'If we can say we want to find Dave real bad, you'd have to say that Arn Lazarus wants him worse than any man alive.'

'I have heard of Lazarus. I thought he was dead.'

'I could name a hell of a lot of people who wish he was,' Quinlan said. 'Dave Cull sure would be among 'em. Head of the list.' He told her what had happened between Cull and Lazarus. 'It would never go away. It would only grow, over time. The name Cull would be enough to draw Lazarus like a buzzard to a carcass. It's something I maybe ought to have thought of, taken account of, an' didn't.'

'What Geddes heard might not be true. It might just be someone speculating.' Quinlan's glance told her what he thought of that opinion. 'How will it affect what we . . . what you do?'

'We don't know where Cull is. Not exactly. We don't know where Lazarus is, therefore how much time we've got. If we're going to get a chance at Cull we'll need to locate him real quick an' get him out. There's no way on God's earth we'd want to run up against Arn Lazarus.'

5

Cull came out of the barn where he had been attending to the roan and ensuring that it had sufficient feed. He would water it soon, then make what farewells there remained time for, and get the hell out of here. Though a seemingly unearthly quiet prevailed all around this place, for Cull, even that had taken on a certain ominous quality. A man who forever must be casting glances over his shoulder, Cull was only too well aware that to light down in one place for long was to invite what could be a dangerous lethargy, a lowering of his guard. Cull, in his time, had known numerous men who had paid for such carelessness with their lives. The trouble was that it was virtually impossible to move any distance, no matter how much care was taken, and escape, totally, the attention of people who immediately talked about who they had seen and when and where. And talk such as that was not confined to ranch or store or saloon; it could travel immense distances in a very short time. And telegraph wires could begin singing, sending words on ahead. No, best be out of here as soon as possible, for there was no more he could do.

Before going back across the yard to the homestead, however, he walked to where the long mound of freshly turned earth was, and picked up the shovel he had used, standing for a few minutes looking at the filled-in grave. There was no marker, not yet. He would not remain here long enough to make one, but would leave extra money with Concepta, to have a proper one made in Abbott's Forge. But only after he was well gone. He must make that quite clear. Wait a week or more.

The coffin he had fashioned himself, from scraps raked up around this one-time farm. Not Cull's farm. Long before his time, the inhabitants had departed, as a result of poor crops, maybe, or poor prices for good crops, or poor advice, or of rampaging diseases or worse men. Whoever they had been, those farm folk, they had left little of themselves behind. A couple of now very old graves up beyond some cottonwoods, the names worn away by the elements, but one, it seemed, from what remained of dates, of a young child.

Cull turned and walked away from the newest grave, restoring the shovel to the barn. When he came out, Concepta was in the yard and he beckoned to her. She came shuffling across, obedient as always, but, as always, leery of him.

'Yuh know what it is you have to do?'

'Si, Señor Cull.'

'Yuh don't move off this place. This here is a safe place.' He hoped to God it was. Lazarus was never far from his mind, even now.

'Si.' She did not look as though she

truly believed any place was safe, where Cull was likely to turn up, or where others might come seeking him. He had given dire warnings about another *gringo* named Lazarus.

'The marker, the proper marker for the grave, that can be made in Abbott's Forge. But yuh wait seven days before yuh go anywhere near there. An' yuh remember what it is yuh tell 'em?'

'Si, Señor Cull. Concepta say she make box for lady. Concepta put in groun' an' she say the words over. Señor Cull, he no come here. No time.'

He stood staring fixedly at her, then fetched a string-pull sack from his pocket and counted out numerous coins, a miscellaneous assortment. Cull said, '*Yanqui* money an' Mex money. Yuh know where there's other money, in the tin box under the floor? Alys's money.'

'Si.'

'I want to know I kin trust yuh, Concepta.'

'You trust.'

Cull gave her another long look, then said, 'Do this for me. Fetch the horse out of the barn an' let him drink. An' fill the canteen.'

'You go now, Señor Cull?'

'I been here too long as it is.' He made to move on by her, then hesitated. 'An' Concepta . . . ?'

'Si?'

'If men should come here, askin', I ain't been here.'

'Men will come?'

'Mebbe. Mebbe not. Cain't never be sure. When I've gone, clean out the barn where the horse was. Git the yard broom an' brush over the tracks. Better still, that ol' hack yuh got in there, walk him around some, make plenty tracks o' his'n.' She nodded, her wide, flat face impassive, her brown-bean eyes watching him as he went pacing away across the hardpack towards the house.

★ ★ ★

67

Lazarus, Jack Guido, Phelps and Lodd, travelling light, no pack-horses, were on the trail, strung out in a line. Lazarus leading, they were pushing ahead at a good pace, a steady pace, not punishing the horses, always on the look-out for habitations, for a sign of humanity anywhere, so that information could be had for the asking.

A couple of cowhands emerging from a small *arroyo* on open range not far from the trail, reined up short at the sight of horsemen, halted, sitting in a half-circle, men who, as the cowhands studied them, began walking their horses forward. The hands were questioned as to what outfit they rode for, and who, if anybody, might have been seen crossing the rangeland or on the trail in recent times. Then Lazarus, whose face these boys were unlikely ever to forget, asked outright if they had heard of anybody called Cull. They shook their heads. One said, 'Nope, never heard o' nobody with that handle, mister.'

'Sure about that, cowboy?'

'Yessir!'

'What's the next town, south?'

'Mendel.'

The other one, perhaps seeking to lighten this abrupt exchange, said, 'Ride through real quick an' yuh'll miss it.'

'Any law there?' This was Guido.

'Nope. Not much o' nothin', mister. Saloon an' some clapped out whores is all.'

Lazarus and his party hauled away and left them gaping, and when far enough away, one of the ranch riders said, 'Dunno who this here Cull kin be, but whoever he is I sure hope he's forkin' a fast animal.'

The town of Mendel was all that had been promised, so they did not tarry there long. There were faces behind windows, watching them ride out.

After a few miles had rolled behind them, Phelps said that if they cut southwest from where they were now, then by morning they ought to be within sight of some small hillocks where there was a natural feature known as Warrior Bluff. For Lazarus had given out his intention of riding on after sundown, even though that meant at a reduced pace. Now that he thought he had a sniff of Dave Cull at long last, he did not intend deviating from his purpose. Nobody saw fit to argue.

* * *

Belle had been installed at the Orion Hotel in Dolomite, a place of near elegance when compared with other establishments of its kind, perhaps a sort of gesture from Quinlan in view of the tensions that had developed on the long and often difficult journey to that place.

Now Abbott's Forge, too, was falling away behind them and there was a sense of urgency, for the Dead River country lay ahead of them. They had divested themselves of two pack-animals in Dolomite, and the third in Abbott's Forge, all to be cared for at liveries against their return and the long haul north, again.

Quinlan thought that the atmosphere among them had improved somewhat since Dolomite and that any tension now and hereafter could be put down to the knowledge that they might be drawing closer to Dave Cull and if so, they did not have any idea of whether, if they found him, they would find him alone. The ugly, dusty shoot all that time ago must have revived itself in each man's mind and, perhaps as Quinlan did, each of them reserved a thought for the dead men they had left in that benighted place. Dave Cull had a lot to answer for, but the day of reckoning could well be at hand. None the less, Quinlan, even to these experienced men, had a word of caution.

'We'll do it the way we agreed we'd do it, the way Bish worked out. We'll split up soon as we get the first wink of the Dead River. From that time on, by God we'd best take it slow an' easy.

If Dave is down there he could see us before we see him. Or he could have men out.' After he had said it, Quinlan wondered if, though they made no response, they thought that being so often with Belle had softened him, while Quinlan in his turn wondered if they were feeling the same twinges of ageing sinews as he was, and were prey to the same uncertainties. Seeing the hard faces looking back at him, he would not have reckoned it to be so.

They angled south-westward now, crossing broken country, much clumped with gnarled, wind-twisted trees and scrawny brush and ruptured with upthrusts of lichen-covered rocks. About once an hour they drew to a halt, and Bishop, dismounting and seeking some slightly elevated place, made a careful, unhurried sweep in every direction with his spyglass. In all of these exercises, all he had to report was a faint run of whitish smoke from a distant locomotive, lying like a long thin feather across the horizon. A couple of hours after that they walked their horses ⸻ a halt and stared ahead. A tiny gleam showed them where the river was, a diamond-like flash among greenery crowding its banks. But distance could be deceptive. It would take them some time yet to reach the river.

Bishop, Naylor and Macafee got down to stretch their legs and to piss. Quinlan sat his saddle, still staring towards where the river was. 'Bish, where's the glass?'

Rebuttoning, Bishop walked to his saddlebags and came and handed the brass spyglass up to Quinlan. 'Somethin'?'

Naylor and Macafee turned their heads, Macafee farting long and loud. 'What's up?'

Quinlan, the extended spyglass to his left eye, did not answer immediately, but when he lowered the glass, said, 'Somebody on the move. Too far to fetch him in with the glass.' Again he looked through the spyglass and this time kept it to his eye for almost a full minute. When he took it away he rubbed a gloved hand at his eye-socket. 'Can't say for sure, but I reckon he's changed direction.' A lone horseman. Quinlan looked again. 'No sign now.' It might mean nothing. It might mean that the glint of the brass spyglass had been seen. Quinlan was in no two minds. If in doubt, assume the worst. Even as he handed the instrument back to Bishop, Naylor and Macafee were remounting. Quinlan extended one arm. 'Cut that way. When we get closer to where I saw him last, we'll spread out in a skirmish-line.'

The fresh interest rippling through the small group was almost palpable. After a long time in the saddle, through nights of uncomfortable, and before Dolomite, often tetchy camps, here at last was something of substance to investigate. They rode on single-mindedly, their line-of-ride tending more westerly than before, each man squinting into the distance, not wanting to miss the merest suggestion of movement. When the thick vegetation that marked the course of the river was clearly in view, Quinlan made the hand-signals which resulted in Macafee heading directly towards the river, Naylor putting distance between himself and Macafee, Bishop and Quinlan also spreading out, finally a good fifty yards between horsemen by the time they all swung to ride towards the river.

They might have spent some time searching and all to no purpose, had a distant horse not commenced whickering. Quinlan waved his arm vigorously, looking left and right, and he and his riders stopped. He waved again, urgently, and they all got down. This was the time to make a careful approach, offering lesser targets. There was no knowing who the horseman was, and if it turned out he was hostile, he could be waiting, concealed in brush, and with a rifle, could drop two of Quinlan's party before you could spit. They unscabbarded their own rifles.

Leading their mounts they walked forward, roughly in the same line-abreast and with similar distance between each man. Again there came the sound of a horse whickering. Again the advancing line stopped. They waited. They were slick with sweat, warmth rising from the earth as much as beating down on their backs. The longer the inactivity and the quiet ran on, the less comfortable did this waiting become. Quinlan was reluctant to move in until he had some better idea of what he was moving in on. Bishop looked across at him and shrugged. Quinlan could see that Bishop had laid his rifle down and was holding the spyglass, waiting for another chance to use it.

Quinlan looked to his left. Dog-faced Naylor, whatever misgivings he might have, was steadfastly fixing his attention on the vegetation at the river. Beyond him, Macafee could be seen likewise singularly occupied. Quinlan turned his head sharply. There had been a sudden rise of small birds from out of the river-trees directly in front of Bishop.

It was maybe a couple of minutes before Bishop pointed and put the spyglass to his eye, for there could now be seen, some thirty yards out in the river, having come into view beyond the fringe of the trees, a man crouching on a strongly swimming horse. All attention now swung to Bishop who alone had the ability to identify the departing rider. But there was no opportunity to do that, not yet anyway.

Bishop, standing with reins wound around one wrist, was tracking the man and the swimming horse until, on the farther bank, the animal, a roan, came heaving out, dripping. It seemed that it would still be all to no avail, that horse and rider would vanish among tall brush and trees there, when the man turned his head to look back. Then he did go in among cover.

Bishop snapped the spyglass shut, calling, 'It's him . . . ! It's Dave Cull . . . !'

6

Pushing through green brush they had put their horses down the bank and into the river, the animals swimming strongly, glad of the coolness, the slow current in some measure pushing at them, wanting to take them gently downstream. They were a little more than halfway across when Cull began shooting at them from cover across on the opposite bank, bullets whipping into the water.

Quinlan pulled his rifle from its scabbard, jacked a round into the chamber and fired at where he had thought he had seen a stir of leaves. Macafee shot too, but immediately had to look to his horse, which seemed set to pitch him off. Long before they reached the farther bank, however, Bishop shouted, 'He's away . . . !'

And so he was, visible now, well

beyond the riverbank brush and soon passing from their view among upthrusts of rock, heading into some much rougher country. Once he was in there they might never see him again.

The horses came heaving out of the water, hooves chopping into soft, grassy earth, blowing, riders urging them up onto comparatively level ground. They went pushing through brush, bursting free then went spurring on, heading for where Cull had last been seen, all now with their rifles free.

Charging between two spearheads of reddish rock, bullets came whining close over them as soon as they arrived in a relatively open space, so they spread out fast, Quinlan shouting for a two-two split, to head towards other rocks on either hand. And Quinlan was making frantic hand-signals to indicate that he wanted all of them to keep pressing ahead, having no wish to become pinned down, made immobile by this single, concealed shooter, even if he was Dave Cull. None the less,

Quinlan was under no illusions. To make a mistake close to any man armed with a rifle was to court disaster. They had just about used up most of their luck already. It was almost unbelievable that at least one of them had not been nailed while they were in the river and moving as though through molasses.

Now they had got into relatively safer cover and were pressing forward, both pairs of hunters, and their boldness was having an effect, a small rise of dust betraying Cull as he hurried to pull back. But it was far from over yet. This was where boldness had to be tempered by caution, as they were very soon to find out.

★ ★ ★

The two bearded itinerants, though still inclined to look over their shoulders because of what had happened at Geddes's Trading Post, never even heard them coming. Sitting cross-legged at a flickering fire, the one who had been buffaloed by Quinlan, and though having bathed his injured head in a creek during the afternoon, was still looking sick and was in some pain. They were not truly rangemen and had been staring into the flames when they heard the cocking of pistols. Looking around proved pointless, for concentrating on the fire had caused them, in the few seconds that counted, to fall prey to night-blindness.

About to start to their feet they were told by Lazarus, stepping into the wavering light, to sit down again. Even when their eyes were again becoming accustomed to the gloom, the men who had come into the clearing were not showing themselves. The nearest one to them, a big man, was the only one they could see, and by no means did they fancy what they saw; even by their own lights, an exceedingly ugly individual, an evil face with very pale, dead eyes — something badly wrong with one of them — a face enough to make a man's belly crawl just looking at it. Lazarus said, 'Keep lookin' at the fire.' They could hear their own sorry-looking mounts whickering as other horses were now fetched in, blowing and clinking. 'Now,' said Lazarus, 'yuh commence tellin' me who yuh are an' what yuh're doin' here.' He had come in close behind them and now touched each on the side of the face with the barrel of the pistol. 'If I don't like what I hear I'll have your stinkin' carcasses pegged out an' set fires on your bellies.'

'Jesus, mister! We ain't doin' no harm to nobody! We been south, an' now we're on the move north ag'in.' And he added an unlikely reason. 'Lookin' fer work.'

The injured man had earlier laid his hat aside, for wearing it had given him discomfort, and now, with the pistol, Lazarus touched the ugly red welt on the man's head, causing him to jump sideways and yell out.

'Some'dy laid a barrel on yuh,'

Lazarus observed.

'Jes' an argyment we had, back down the trail a-ways, is all.'

'An argyment with who, and what about?'

'Didn't know the feller from Adam.'

'By the looks,' said another voice (Guido's), 'yuh won't fergit the bastard in a hurry.'

The other man at the fire said, 'We couldn't do nothin'. There was pistols on us. An' there was four o' the bastards.'

'Where?'

'At the tradin' post.'

'Geddes's?'

'Yeah, reckon so.'

'These four,' Lazarus said, 'tell me about 'em.'

'Never clapped eyes on any of 'em afore.'

'And with no names,' said Lazarus.

'Yeah.' Suddenly the seated man's beard was seized and his head wrenched around so fiercely that he thought his neck would snap. '*Jesus* . . . !'

'Remember some names, mister,' Lazarus said. He let the man's beard go.

'Christ, mister, I went outside! They was talkin' to Geddes.'

Lazarus tapped the other man on the cheek with the pistol, and none too gently. 'Yuh go outside?'

'They was askin' Geddes if he'd seen a feller called Cull.'

A silence fell and to the two at the fire there was a sense that other men were coming closer in behind them, to listen. In a softer voice, Lazarus asked, 'An' what did fat Geddes have to say to that?'

'Christ, mister, I never heeard it all. I was down the store a-ways. But I did hear Geddes say he hadn't seen this Cull.'

Again there was a silence, then somebody coughed. After a few more seconds, Lazarus said, 'Tell me about these men that was doin' this askin'. Four, yuh say?'

'Yeah. An' one woman.'

'A *woman?*'

'Yeah. Real good-lookin' woman she was. Buxom. She didn't say nothin'. Not that I heard. But she sure come in with 'em an' she was there when we pulled out.'

'Names,' Lazarus said.

'On'y two,' the man at the fire said. 'I kin recall but one of 'em, and that's God's truth, mister. The one that sounded like the head rooster, he said to Geddes, he said, *yuh know Mr Bishop.*'

There was a certain stirring among those standing behind. One man said, '*Shit!*'

'Bishop,' said Lazarus.

'That's the on'y one I recall.'

'By any chance,' Lazarus asked, almost lazily, 'would the other name have been Quinlan?'

'By God, that's it . . . ! Sure is! Quinlan.' That was absorbed with some stirring, too.

'No more names?'

'No, mister, an' I ain't lyin' to yuh.'

'I believe yuh,' said Lazarus, sounding, for the first time, reasonable.

The man who had been answering looked relieved. That was when Lazarus nodded to Guido, who extended his pistol, and together they blew the brains of both itinerants into the fire.

* * *

The fierce fight, with rifles, was going on among old rocks, granules flying from striking lead that often went whining away above crouching men. The heat had become unpleasant, exacerbated by the presence of so much rock, so that the river, glinting some distance behind them, was a constant, tantalizing temptation.

Quinlan's group was still divided, and Quinlan and Bishop, on the right, were slightly ahead of Naylor and Macafee. Cull, seen only in brief, sudden glimpses, afoot now, presumably having got his horse tied somewhere nearby, was also gradually rctreating, but there had been ample evidence that he was highly dangerous. The bastard sure could shoot.

The Quinlan horses had been picketed in sparse brush some hundred yards back, out of sight, when the vulnerability of men mounted became patently obvious. Clearly, though, this business of the horses was now of some concern to Bishop.

'He draws us too far from the horses, an' then he remounts, we could lose him.'

That had been going through Quinlan's mind, too, and he had in mind to call out to Macafee to go back and fetch the horses forward; but he had held back because he did not want to risk Cull overhearing what was going on. There was more shooting, then a lull. Hardly had Quinlan commented on the horses to Bishop than there was another lashing of shots from where Cull was, and in a flurry of dust and kicked pebbles, Naylor arrived, sweaty and dusty, his long face in a serious cast.

'Mac got hit. He's real bad. I done what I could but he won't last.'

Quinlan slapped the stock of his rifle. Not much time would pass before he began blaming himself for what had happened to Macafee, but at almost the same instant, in looking up, he caught sight of Cull, on his horse, racing across a gap towards further, probably better, cover. Quinlan up and tracked the running animal and shot. The horse screamed and threw its head up, its hindquarters seeming to be dragging, and its rider went rolling off it. Quinlan shot again and this time struck the horse in the head and it crashed down dustily.

'There . . . !' Naylor shouted. It was Cull, apparently unhurt and running bent over, heading for the rocky cover he had not been able to reach on the horse.

Bishop shot at him, and while in full flight Cull was punched sideways, then was down and rolling. When the rise of dust dissipated he could be seen on hands and knees, still managing to take his rifle with him, still going doggedly towards his objective. Bishop shot again and hit him again, and Cull pitched down on his face and moved no more. His hat had come off when he fell.

They waited to make sure where his rifle was before Quinlan said, 'Move in,' and they rose and went, all three, up the very slight incline, rifles at hip, until they were about thirty feet from where he lay. His rifle had been flung some four feet in front of him. Cull had a pistol strapped on but his right hand was nowhere near it. Now their rifles were being held butt-plate-to-shoulder as they walked to him. He was not dead. He was quivering and making a choking noise. Naylor and Bishop continued pointing their rifles at him while Quinlan laid his aside and went to kneel on one knee next to Cull.

The first thing that Quinlan did, working at it, was to draw Cull's pistol from him, then spin it across the ground towards Bishop. Carefully, Naylor came circling around and picked up Cull's rifle and took it further away. Quinlan managed to get Cull turned over. There was a lot of blood on him and some was now on Quinlan. Naylor said, 'I got to go take a look at Mac. Then I'll fetch the mounts up.' They heard his boots scuffing as he went trudging away.

Cull's horse was making spasming leg movement and rasping noises. Bishop went to it and his rifle lashed as he put the animal down.

Cull, in a low, short-of-breath voice, was trying to focus on the man kneeling near him, but it seemed to be beyond him to do so.

'Who . . . are yuh?'

'Tom Quinlan.'

It could have been a slight nod of the head but was not, quite, merely a closing and reopening of eyes. Cull was badly shot. The first one had gone into his right side, high on the chest, the next just beneath the right shoulder blade. There was blood everywhere, all

90

over his upper clothing, and now a bright red had appeared on his lower lip and run down his chin. For all the ravages of the grievous wounds he had suffered, Cull still appeared as a fine-looking man, and there would sure be a string of women across the country who would lament his passing. But he was a rawhide-tough man, too, and he was not dead yet.

* * *

Pat Geddes had backed off behind his counter as far as he could manage to get, but Jack Guido placed one sinewy hand on the planking and vaulted over. Geddes would have retreated along the length of the counter but Guido reached and seized him near the top of the grubby undervest. Guido said, 'Move one more time, yuh fat bag o' shit, an' we'll take yuh out an' bust your laigs. Then yuh won't move far.'

Geddes knew damn' well that they would do it, too. You had but to look at the bastards, and knowing that the ugliest of the four and the biggest among them really was Arn Lazarus, a man he had seen before, Geddes had near to shit himself where he stood.

They were all inside, Josh Phelps as well, and Asa Lodd, him leaning in the open doorway, arms folded. Lazarus, both of his broad hands propped against the edge of the counter said, 'Listen to what I say, fat man. I ain't got no time to stand jawin'. We know Tom Quinlan's been here, an' Bishop, an' two more, an' some woman.' And while he knew the answer to his own question, he must have thought to test Geddes. 'What did Quinlan want?'

'He come in askin' fer Dave Cull.'

'What did yuh say to Quinlan?'

'That Cull ain't been in here, an' he ain't.'

The strange, pale eyes had settled unmovingly on Geddes, and Jack Guido was still standing alongside him. Guido said, 'This polecat's prob'ly lyin', Arn.'

'I ain't!' said Geddes, his voice going

high. 'Why would som'dy like Dave Cull come in here?'

There was a certain logic to that, as Lazarus must have known, so he changed his enquiry. 'Quinlan. Bishop. Who was the others?'

'Never seen 'em afore,' said Geddes, 'an' nobody give out no names. The woman, I never seen neither.'

Lazarus began pacing around, not looking at merchandise but obviously thinking, scheming. Lazarus had begun to get the mad animal look about him, probably because of these complications, these frustrations. Quinlan. Bishop. Two other men. And there was now no doubt at all that they were out seeking Cull, and they were ahead of him — Lazarus — by some good distance. He came pacing back to face Geddes. 'How many horses?'

'Seven. Three pack-animals.'

That seemed a lot. 'All well loaded?'

'Nope. Plenty o' stuff, but well spread across the three.'

That was more like it. If they had

come a good distance and wanted to do it in good time, they would not want heavily loaded animals. They would be seeking to maintain a good, steady pace. Lazarus nodded, and to Geddes's immense relief, made a sign to Guido, who came back over the counter, and they all went outside.

Mounting up, Lazarus, his voice lowered, said, 'Next town is Dolomite. We'll not stop there. We're a long ways back. There's time to make up.'

* * *

Naylor had not come back from Macafee and had not fetched the horses in. Bishop said he would go find out what was happening.

Cull was still hanging on. He sure had some sand, Quinlan thought, Cull even asking, 'Which one o' yuh was it? You?'

'No. Kel Bishop.'

Momentarily Cull's eyes closed. 'Mighta . . . knowed it.'

'If it hadn't been one of us,' Quinlan said, 'it would've been somebody else. You weren't being careful enough. It could well have been Arn Lazarus.'

The effect the words had on the mortally wounded Cull was startling. He even made an attempt to struggle to a sitting position, but of course failed. Plainly, though, he had become highly agitated at the sound of Lazarus's name. Now he did manage, just, to say, 'Where . . . ?'

'Geddes, at the trading post, he reckons Arn's on the move. I don't know where.'

Cull's breathing was shortening, but limply, with one hand, he made Quinlan understand that he wanted to say something. Quinlan bent down, his ear almost touching Cull's bloodied mouth.

It was almost five minutes before Bishop and Naylor came back, leading the horses. Naylor, looking somewhat sourly at Quinlan, said, 'Mac's done for.'

'So's Dave Cull.'

They stood looking at the dead man, flies beginning to dart over his face.

'So, that's that,' Bishop said. He shoved his hat back. 'Now we got to get the both of 'em covered up. Then we can get the hell out of here an' on back to Dolomite. We can telegraph from there, let 'em know it's done.'

'Three-way split now,' Naylor mumbled sombrely. 'Mac didn't have nobody.' Naylor was looking at Quinlan as though he had come to the view that what had happened to Macafee was probably the dire result of Quinlan's rushing things. Now Naylor knew who it had been that he had felt was on the trail, behind them all the way. It had been Death.

'It's not quite done with yet,' Quinlan said. 'Well, not for me. You'll have to decide.'

Then he told them what Dave Cull had said to him and what, in turn, he had said to Cull.

7

She was in her room but had not gone to bed. By lamplight she had been reading the *Dolomite Echo* and not finding anything to engage her interest. By this time she had become sharply on edge. She hated the name of Cull and had come to dislike the names of Naylor, of Macafee and even of Bishop, a man who had sometimes gone out of his way to be thoughtful of what he reckoned were her needs at various times. Most of all she was annoyed by the name of Quinlan. She was in fact in the third stage of anxious waiting, the first having been her own professed indifference, on the eve of their departure, the second, the recurring fears over recent days that it might all have gone wrong, the third, anger. And the more corrosive for the fact that there was no-one here to vent it on. During the lonely, seemingly endless hours, she had even begun to wonder if she and Quinlan might have come to the end of things. Remember Naylor. What she had wanted Quinlan to do was confront the man, demand that he say outright if her presence presented a real problem for him. Quinlan had not done it. She knew quite well that it was not because he was afraid of Naylor. More likely it was because he had no wish to introduce a note of disharmony, early on in that enterprise. That had put her, Belle, firmly in the second rank. She had just stood up and put the newspaper aside when the tapping on the door told her that he was back. His special tap.

When Quinlan opened the door, stepped inside and closed it again, she did not move. There was no immediate embrace, only a silent scrutiny. It seemed that he was unhurt. His hat, which he was holding in one hand, he tossed onto a chair, and moved closer, the light from a lamp disclosing his unkempt appearance, his dusty clothes and several days' growth of black whiskers which, along with his black, hanging moustache, made him look inordinately swarthy. His cheeks were sunken and his eyes red-rimmed and dulled with weariness and, she thought, a certain defeat.

Some of her anger had drained away, but there was, none the less, an edge in her voice when she said, 'You've been longer than I thought you'd be.'

He nodded, rubbed at and finger-massaged the back of his neck. 'We had to come part of the way back by a longer route.'

'You've brought Dave Cull in?'

Slowly Quinlan shook his head. 'Dave's dead. He left us no choice. It cost us, too. Mac's dead. They're both buried at a place across the Dead River.'

She absorbed this litany of death in silence. It was almost half a minute before she said, 'I knew how dangerous Dave Cull was, but

99

somehow I didn't expect you to lose anybody. Considering who was in the party. Did you?'

'You can never predict what will happen. A whole lot of things can come into it. Maybe it comes down to how I went about things when we were pressing Dave real hard. I reckon Naylor thinks so. He's moved on already, taken one of the pack-horses, the one we picked up at Abbott's Forge.'

'So you did come through there?'

'Yes, to get that horse, but we took a wide circle around to get to the place.'

'Why?'

'First, because of what Geddes said about Lazarus. That got more complicated. Arn will still be coming.'

'You mean because he doesn't know that Cull's dead?'

'He might well have found that out by now. I'd just about put money on it.'

'Well, surely that would be an end of it.'

'I got to talk with Dave, some. After he was shot,' Quinlan sighed. 'I told him about Arn Lazarus being out. He took it hard. He was sure Lazarus wouldn't let it go.' Realizing he was confusing her, he said, 'Dave's wife was dead. That's why he was where he was.'

'His *wife*?'

Quinlan nodded. 'So it seems.'

'Well, he couldn't have been concerned for *her* safety.'

'No. But he sure was for his girl's.' Quinlan stood blinking at her. 'His daughter.'

Belle stared at him. 'Did you know Dave Cull had a daughter?'

'No. I knew he was supposed to have women all over the place. But I didn't know about the wife or the daughter. They were at an abandoned farm 'way down there. Out-of-the-way place. The girl, the mother an' an old Mexican woman. Cook, nurse, whatever was needed. I don't know how long they'd been there or how often Cull might have gone there in the past.'

'But Cull told you all about them?'

'Yes. An' we went there, to the farm.' Quinlan rubbed slowly at his eyelids. 'Dave was worried . . . No, more than worried. He was terrified Lazarus would find the farm. Find her.'

'And so he might, I expect.'

Quinlan said, 'Lazarus might find the farm. He'll not find the girl there.'

'Where is she?'

'In this hotel. In a room along the hall. I brought her in on Mac's horse.'

For several seconds, Belle apparently could not trust herself to speak. Then, 'You brought her *here*?'

'I reckoned I could hardly leave her where she was. Not in all the circumstances.' *I*, he had said. Did that mean that neither Naylor nor Bishop had wanted a part of it?

Skirts rustling, Belle walked across the room to a chair and sat down. 'Tom, I'm finding it hard to get to grips with this. What happens now? To her? Where does she go from here?'

Though he must have been bone weary and in need of a hot tub and many hours of sleep, he did not sit down but started moving around the room almost as though he did not know how to go on.

'Dave told me there's a woman lives in Morwenna, some kin of his wife's, I gather, named Hattie Nelson. I promised Dave I'd take the girl there, to that woman. He reckoned Hattie Nelson could be persuaded to take her east from there, well out of harm's way.'

'You *what*?' Then, without waiting for him to say anything, she said, '*Girl*? How old is she?'

'Sixteen, about.'

Belle stood up, face colouring. 'I don't believe what I'm hearing. You are telling me that you've given an undertaking, to an outlaw, a man who's known to have taken I don't know how many lives, a drunken womanizer and

God alone knows what else besides, to traipse all over the country with a female who is little more than a child, who you'd never clapped eyes on before and who, in all likelihood, is carrying the exact same brand as her father?'

Quinlan had expected some protest, but the slight lift of his head indicated that the intensity of Belle's outburst had taken him by surprise. But he recovered. 'I told a dying man I'd do the best I could for his daughter, before Arn Lazarus got wind of her.' He paused, then added, 'I'd not want to think of Arn getting his hands on her, or any other girl, a Cull or not.'

Belle was breathing deeply, her breast rising and falling. 'And this other woman, the Mexican woman, I expect you brought her along too.'

Quinlan shook his head. 'She refused to come. She plans to head further south, through New Mexico and across the border, to her own people.'

'But she knows who you are, who it is who's taken Cull's daughter? So, does she know *where* you're taking her, or where you might *be*, right now?'

'No. I told the girl, convinced her that her pa wanted her to get right away from that farm. But I didn't say anything about Morwenna 'til we were on the journey; nor Dolomite, but Lazarus is real cunning. Foxy. I can't take chances.'

'So now you're going to Morwenna.'

'Yeah. I thought you could go on with Bish, up through Mendel to Carver, the way we came. Take one of the pack-horses. I'll take the other.'

'So, that's me tidily put away. Again. What does Bish think about all this?'

Now Quinlan was somewhat irritated. 'If you'd rather travel all that way on your own, then do it. I wouldn't recommend it. It was . . . '

'I know! *I* wanted to come as far as Dolomite. It was *my* doing. I've got nobody to blame but myself.' When he merely stared at her, she said, 'And now this . . . girl of Dave Cull's, what did *she* say when you said you'd take

105

her to Morwenna? It would have to be across some of the worst country in five hundred miles. You could have put her on the train here in Dolomite, except there's no rail-road that goes near Morwenna.'

'Nor any stage-line from here,' Quinlan said. 'Don't you think I've been over all that in my mind?'

'What *did* she say? *'Thank you kindly, Mr Quinlan, and by the way, was it your bullet killed my Pa?'* '

'No. An' as a matter of fact, it was a couple of Bish's shots.'

'I expect that absolves you.'

'She knew it was always a possibility that her pa would get in a fight that he couldn't walk out of. We took him to the farm an' we buried him there, right next to where he'd buried his wife. We decided to bury Mac there, as well.'

'And she went through all that and agreed to all this, and said nothing?'

'That's right. She has good sight an' good hearing an' looks normal in every way, but she can't speak.

She's never been able to speak.' That did shake Belle. Quinlan went on, 'She can understand an' make herself understood. Her ma taught her. She can read an' write a lot better than most. She showed us while we were at the farm, explaining to the old Mex woman what had happened, an' about Lazarus an' what Dave wanted us to do.' Us, now, Belle thought sourly.

'I see. Do I get to meet this . . . clever young female?'

'Of course. But in the morning.'

'And who's paying for that hotel room? You?'

'No. There was some money — hers — at the farm. She's not destitute. But she gave some to the old woman.'

'I wonder how she came by that money? From Dave Cull, no doubt. The fruits of some terrible mischief or other. Dead men's money, maybe?'

'Look, Belle, there's a hell of a lot of things could be made out of this. But whatever Cull was, an' whatever he did, that's not been her fault. She's entitled to live an' be given a chance. She didn't apply to be Dave Cull's daughter.'

'You've only got Cull's say-so that Lazarus would want to do her harm.'

'I believed him.'

From the hot look on her face it seemed she was about to launch a fresh attack but in the event was interrupted by a tapping on the door. An employee of the hotel, calling, 'Mr Quinlan?'

'Yes?'

'Sheriff Olman's down in the lobby, Mr Quinlan . . . wants a word . . . '

'I'll be down,' Quinlan called.

'Now what?'

Quinlan picked up his hat and put it on. 'Maybe he's come to arrest me.'

'Or her.'

Quinlan left, closing the door behind him.

In the amber-lit lobby stood a wide-shouldered, plump-faced man in a broadcloth suit, a badge on the left lapel, and he had on a narrow-brimmed townsman's hat. If he was armed, it was not evident.

'Mr Quinlan?'

'Yeah.'

'Jake Olman, Dolomite County. Heard you'd come in . . . Saw you, as a matter of fact.'

The clerk, behind his counter, was standing, big-eyed and attentive, so Quinlan said, 'Sheriff, why don't we step outside?'

Olman, his mouth open, about to say something else, seemed knocked slightly off balance, but went tramping outside behind Quinlan, onto the boardwalk.

'Mr Quinlan, we've not met before, but of course I've heard of you.' Clearly he had got a lot more word on the wind or the wire, or both, for he came right to the point. 'I've heard you're out after Dave Cull.' The word, wherever it had come from, was now out of date.

'We already caught up with Dave in country on the other side of the Dead River. We exchanged fire with rifles. Cull opened up first. He was shot, an' died a short time after. We also lost one of our party, Mr Macafee.' It sounded like some kind of official report.

Olman's lips were pressed firmly together, an act seeming to widen his round face. 'My! Dave Cull, dead! Well now, there's a thing.' Then, 'I saw a girl come in with you, very young-looking.'

'Cull's daughter. The surviving close relative. His wife's dead. That's the reason he came to the surface after all this time out of sight, an' headed down there.'

Olman looked nearly as surprised as Belle had. He ventured, 'You've, er, taken charge of her?'

'Only for a time. I'm taking her on from here, seeing her safe to a kinswoman. Right now she's resting up. She's been through a lot. Arn Lazarus was out after Dave as well. Failing to kill Dave, he'll want this young lady's ears for his belt. So Dave claimed, an' (as he had said to Belle) I believed him.'

'Arn Lazarus! By God, you mean there's some chance Lazarus will come here looking for her?'

'I can't know that. I have to assume he will.'

Whatever impulse had brought Olman here in the first place, curiosity, a show of official efficiency perhaps, had quickly been overpowered by the mention of Arn Lazarus.

'Now look here, Mr Quinlan, I can't prevent you passing through this county or this town.' Then he said, 'I also take care of what a marshal would do, in the town, if we had one. But I have to tell you this: I can't risk Lazarus coming in here an' causing a ruckus. He'll be bound to have other scallawags along. Anyway, I don't have the firepower for it.'

Quinlan, now getting tired of the man, said, 'There must be plenty of dodgers in your office with Lazarus's face on 'em. For years, Arn's been a wanted man, all over. Think of the kudos if you arrest him.'

Olman's big face coloured darkly. 'Just you get her gone from here, Quinlan. That's my word, now. Get her gone.'

'She'll go,' said Quinlan, 'an' I'll go, as soon as we're rested up.'

Suddenly Olman asked, 'Where are you taking her?' Thinking of words perhaps singing along the wire, Quinlan said,

'That's my business, an' Miss Cull's. I'm not saying, an' I can tell you she's not, either.' Quinlan turned and went back inside the lobby of the Orion.

Soon, Belle asked, 'What did he want?'

'I'm still not sure,' Quinlan said, 'but he got more than he bargained for. It's surprising what the name Arn Lazarus will do to all kinds of people.' Which did not mean that he was about to begin taking Arn Lazarus cheaply.

★ ★ ★

Asa Lodd with his long-jawed face called to them as he came jouncing back, having ridden off to the right, up onto a small plateau, from which place the view was less restricted by vegetation.

Lazarus, Josh Phelps and Jack Guido turned their horses in his direction, then as they drew closer, Lodd called, 'Some kind o' sodbuster outfit. Mebbe no bastard there. Sure don't look like it.'

When they all got to where they could observe the seemingly abandoned farm, they drew rein, Lazarus wishing to study it. The minutes went by.

Presently a woman, an old woman judging by the way she was walking, came out of the barn and went across the yard to the homestead. She did not even glance in the direction of the mounted men. Lazarus, his pale eyes quite still, slowly took in every detail of the place. The horses, some shaking heads and flicking ears, were shifting slightly under their riders.

Finally, Lazarus said, 'Not an animal in sight. Not a Goddamn' chicken, an' no crop planted in God knows how long. Why would anybody want to live in a dump like this?' When no reasons were offered, he said, 'So let's git on down an' find out.'

8

Alys Lilian Cull was sixteen years old, five feet four inches in height, very slim, but small and softly rounded. She had skin like cream silk, dark hair, centre-parted and falling thickly to the small of her back. Her face was heart-shaped, her lips full and pink, but her most striking feature was the colour of her large eyes, a deep violet.

When Belle first set *her* eyes on this slim-armed, dainty creature with her narrow hands and long fingers, just how expressive those hands were was yet to be demonstrated. For Alys, introduced by Quinlan to Belle, in a room at the Orion Hotel, seemed shy to the point of being overwhelmed and, the introduction over, stood with her eyes downcast and her hands clasped in front of her, as though striking an attitude consistent with being paraded for inspection. She had on a yellow and white gingham dress, one of the several articles of clothing that Quinlan had allowed her time to pack before leaving the derelict farm, a garment that hugged her young body and accentuated the smallness of her waist.

Quinlan brought forward a chair and Alys sat down, smiling at him and nodding. Belle found her own chair. The child-woman who had been led in was much too striking-looking. Flowers such as this one seated before her surely did not open to the sun in deserted homesteads south of the Dead River, nor have even the remotest connection with a known killer.

Quinlan did not stand, as so often he preferred to do, but placed a chair alongside Alys Cull and sat down. Belle stared at him but the expression on his hard, heavily moustached face was unreadable. If Belle was, for the present, put off balance and unsure yet what to make of her, Alys Cull, though she did not show it, but would convey thoughts on it to Quinlan at a later time, knew, instantly, that the other woman did not like her and certainly did not like her being anywhere near Quinlan. It was absurd. He was a man near middle age, widely regarded as nobody's fool, Alys scarcely more than a child. Belle was certainly reading more into it than some ridiculous promise that Quinlan had made to a dying felon. As soon as she had gathered herself, Belle began addressing herself to Alys.

'So, Miss Cull, you've been living somewhere south of the Dead River?' It was perhaps said more loudly than Belle had intended, betraying the common misapprehension among those with all their faculties that others, impaired in vision, speech or the movement of limbs, are also hard of hearing.

The first response by Alys was a fleeting touch she gave her small ears, very quick indeed, merely something in passing, before nodding to Belle. A faint colour had come into Belle's cheeks. She knew that she had been mildly rebuked. '*I can hear just fine.*' Quinlan was looking at the floor. At that instant Belle could cheerfully have cut his throat. Then, in a reduced voice, Belle told the girl that she was indeed sorry to hear the news of her mother's death, and asked, 'Was she your teacher?'

A brief nod, a rapid touch of eyes and ears, a miming of reading and writing. Belle sat back slowly, no doubt taken by surprise by the rapidity of the response and its clarity, the animation of the girl, fingers, hands, arms, eyes, a tilt of head, delicate eyebrows raised, all working together to convey her meaning. It was an unpretentious performance, emerging without hesitation, the fruits of long practice, so that it had seemed to be second nature. Suddenly, turning to Quinlan, Alys made other signs, also plain enough for Belle to understand.

Quinlan stood and crossed to a walnut bureau and brought from a drawer a sheet of paper and a pencil.

Alys took them from him and went to a small side-table and wrote something down. She handed the paper to Quinlan who read what she had written, then handed the sheet to Belle. Belle read the small, even, stylish script. '*My mother taught school in Montana and Arizona. That was before I was born.*' Raising one of her hands '*Wait.*' She slipped out of the room and very soon came back with a small, metal-framed photograph which she must have wrapped among her things before leaving the farm. She gave it to Quinlan who studied it for a time before passing it to Belle. It showed a group of three people, taken in a studio, a handsome man in a Sunday best broadcloth suit, standing behind the chair of a lovely, dark-haired woman, a child of perhaps seven standing alongside her. Dave Cull, his wife and his daughter, Alys. Belle looked from the photograph (A. Drucker, Laramie) to the girl. There could be no doubt that she was the same as the one in the picture.

Alys had resumed her seat but Quinlan remained standing. He was wondering what in God's name could have brought a schoolteacher, an educated woman, possibly from an equally educated family, into a liaison with a man such as Dave Cull. Handsome though he might have been and possessing what was customarily referred to as *a way with women*, did that same woman know all that there was to know about him, before marriage, or did she only come to a shocking realization afterwards? That Cull had thought enough of her to risk his own life in coming to her when she was dying, was something that Quinlan was still surprised about. Cull's being drawn back to this astonishing girl might have been a large part of it. The agonized look that had been in the man's clouding eyes during the last minutes of his life was still vivid in Quinlan's mind. There was a rap on the door and Bishop's voice called, seeking Quinlan.

Quinlan said, 'Come on in.'

Bishop came in, his shrewd eyes flicking between Alys Cull and Belle. Quinlan indicated a chair but Bishop, who was holding his hat, shook his head. He had come to discuss the final arrangements for leaving Dolomite and to become clear in his own mind about where it was that Quinlan intended splitting away to head for Morwenna with this girl, and perhaps what was equally important, what Belle's feelings were on this whole question of Belle going on with him, Bishop, to Carver, she to wait there for Quinlan.

Belle said, 'I think you know my views already.'

* * *

Jack Guido and Asa Lodd had been going about emptying drawers and looking through cupboards, and now various floors were strewn with clothing and all manner of miscellaneous articles. Guido, trailed by Lodd, now emerged from the homestead. Lazarus and Phelps were in the yard. They had the old woman, Concepta, there as well. Her mouth was already bloodied, for, to Lazarus's questions she had only unleashed a rapid stream of Spanish.

In one hand Guido had a framed photograph (the glass starred because Lodd's boot had trodden on it) and this he showed to Lazarus and Phelps. It was of two females (head and shoulders), an exceptionally good-looking woman and a very pretty child, clearly the daughter. Lazarus took a long look at it before throwing it down. He walked away, punching a fist into the gloved palm of his other hand. Lodd asked, 'What now?'

Phelps and Guido, boots planted apart, stood waiting, watching Lazarus, seeing the tense, urgent set of him as he paced. To Phelps, Guido said, 'This ol' Spic no use?'

'She don't seem to know our lingo.'

Lazarus turned on his heel and came back towards them. 'We don't know that fer sure.' Then, 'Watch that ol' crow.' He went around the yard looking inside the various old outbuildings. It was not long before he returned carrying a rust-gingered steel rod some three feet in length and an inch square, a remnant of some long-gone piece of farm apparatus, a pump maybe. 'We're gonna find out what lingos she knows. Start a fire.'

* * *

Quinlan had used the back of the paper that Alys had written on to draw a rough map, and now he and Bishop stood looking at it.

'We'll all leave here together,' Quinlan said. 'It seems to me I'll have to head off before we get as far as Mendel, or the going'll be too tough for Alys.'

'Wherever you do it, you'll sure find it slow going,' Bishop observed. 'You'll have to pick your way through the hills there, some ravines, an' all that timber an' big rock.'

123

'I don't see I have any choice. Anyway, every hour that passes could be bringing Arn closer to us. I can't risk her.' Bishop knew what was in Quinlan's mind. Slow going it might be in that unappealing terrain, but once in there the better the concealment from pursuers.

Belle raised the next question, which was not surprising. 'Suppose Lazarus catches up with *us* before we get as far as Carver? If he does come this way he'll soon know that we all rode out of Dolomite together. If he goes on to Mendel, the word will be that only two of us passed through there.'

'By then it'll be too late to catch up with either pair of us. Mind you, we'll need to move along soon.'

'Then by your calculations, we should be well in the clear?'

'That's as I see it.'

Bishop was pensive. His expression could have been saying that he did not easily accept that. Things could go wrong, anytime, no matter what plans happened to be. And there was something else. Perhaps, at some later time, and if anything *did* go amiss, he might be seen as having gone scuttling away, leaving Quinlan with the real difficult task, even if it had been Quinlan alone who had chosen to do it. Kel Bishop and Tom Quinlan went back a long way. In more than one Godforsaken dump they had walked through the smoke together, and now these odd circumstances, the presence of the two women in particular, woven into what had been and still was a most dangerous enterprise, had presented Bishop with choices he would rather not have had to make. At one point he had even considered proposing that all four should head off into that bad country, to take the Cull girl to Morwenna, so that he might be there to lend strong support to Quinlan if the need should arise. But Bishop knew that Belle would never have a bar of it. The mounting antipathy between her and Quinlan over the commitment to

Cull was palpable. Bishop had formed the impression that a whole lot more would have been passing between them had he and Alys not been in the room. Belle, as he knew, could be a strong-minded woman. The fact that she had insisted on coming as far as Dolomite was testament enough to that. So, in a sense, if Belle believed that there were difficulties confronting her now, then they had been of her own making. All of which did not alter the fact that they must all watch their backs and that he, Bishop, had the responsibility of getting Belle safe to Carver. Thereafter, once Quinlan had reappeared, he, Bishop, must press on elsewhere, to transact other business which he had not chosen to elaborate on.

Alys had been sitting listening to the talk. Belle had been studying her. The girl now reached out to touch Quinlan's sleeve. When he looked Alys made quick gestures that included him and Belle and herself. There could be no misreading. *'I am the cause of trouble between you.*' So there it was, fetched *out* into the open by a girl who could not even speak. After a slight doubt, Quinlan thought it was possibly for the best. The skirmish-and-run and skirmish-again pattern which had so often formed between Belle and himself was certainly not to his liking. He said, 'Alys, I gave your pa my word I'd take you to where Hattie Nelson is. I'll get that done an' then I'll meet Belle again, up in Carver. We've all agreed on it.'

That left the way open for Belle to attack him, but something that was hanging in the atmosphere gave her pause. She said, 'Alys, what Mr Quinlan says is right. You mustn't be allowed to fall into the hands of Arn Lazarus. I understand that.'

Even Bishop looked slightly surprised. It was by no means what he had expected. Maybe Belle had come to the view that there was no point in resisting, publicly, but would reserve her true feelings for Quinlan's ears alone.

* * *

Phelps and Lodd brought the horses forward, having watered them, and now all was urgency, Lazarus chivvying them along for the run to Abbott's Forge, then on to Dolomite, for that was the way Lazarus thought they would have gone. That was the only thing that he had been left to guess.

One end wrapped in water-soaked rags torn from Concepta's clothing, the steel shaft lay, still glowing dully, on the hardpack near the smouldering fire. There was a stench in the air that the horses did not like, and they took some settling before all four men were mounted.

From the heavy hoist-beam jutting from the old barn, hung, head down, the naked body of the old woman, her still-dark, unpinned hair almost touching the ground, her breasts like punctured melons. The body was turning slowly on the rope. There were ugly red and black burns on it.

The first had been the one on the lower belly, the one upon which she had rediscovered the ability to speak to them in English. Another deep burn in the left groin had revealed all there was to know about Dave Cull, his much more circumspect comings and goings in the past, to this last visit to his dying wife when perhaps, through anxiety, he had not taken sufficient care and had paid for that with his own life. The burn to the left breast that had destroyed the nipple had brought forth the revelation of Alys Cull. The iron pressed to the sole of the left foot had given them the name of Quinlan, but not those of the two bitter-faced men with him, nor that of the fourth, the dead one, fetched in with Cull and buried at this farm. But no amount of burning, bringing again and again the stench of seared flesh, could reveal to them the details of the route to be taken by Quinlan and his men and Alys Cull, for this Concepta had not been told. So she had died screaming

129

that she did not know.

Arn Lazarus, Joshua Phelps, Asa Lodd and Jack Guido now departed from that place of ugly death, spurring their horses into a strong gallop. They would ride, Lazarus said, without pausing except to let the animals blow, until they ran the Quinlan party down.

9

Olman, the Dolomite County Sheriff, was like a blowfly in an outhouse. Quinlan was on his way to the livery where all their horses had been installed, and Olman, clearly a morning-walker and a looker-into-things, and who obviously had been on the lookout for Quinlan, caught sight of him. Waiting for a wagon to pass by, Olman now came angling quickly across the main street, badge winking in the insipid sunlight. Quinlan would not have paused had not Olman called and come striding to him.

'Mr Quinlan, I got to know now what your plans are.'

'My plans haven't changed since last time we talked.'

'Am I to understand from that,' Olman asked, 'that your, er, people are not yet rested enough to travel?'

Today he was armed. The coat of his broadcloth suit was unbuttoned and the handle of what could have been a Colt Lightning was visible, the pistol holstered in reverse on his left hip.

Before Quinlan could say anything more, their attention was drawn to the appearance, further along the street, of two women; Alys Cull and Belle. Belle either did not see Quinlan or chose to ignore him, and soon both she and Alys vanished inside one of the stores.

'Cull's girl,' murmured Olman.

'Indeed she is,' said Quinlan, and could not hold back from adding, smiling slightly, 'The meat that maybe will draw the scavengers into this county of yours, Sheriff.'

Olman did not smile. 'I've got people I'm committed to protect, Mr Quinlan. I don't want Arn Lazarus coming here.' Then, 'I take it he's not riding alone. Who's with him?'

Quinlan said he did not know. 'If I had to guess, I'd say one of 'em would likely be Jack Guido.'

Olman's round face was doughy-looking. There could be no question but that he would know the implications of that. 'I'll say again what I said before. I can't risk Lazarus coming in here an' causing trouble.' Now he added, 'I've got but two deputies to cover this entire county.'

'I'm sure, like all of us, you've got your problems, Sheriff, an' I sure don't take all of this lightly. Just as soon as may be, we'll all ride out of here. But I've got two women to look to, an' I'll want to be sure they're ready for what's going to be a tough ride.' He did not offer Olman any details, much less give any hint that the party of four which was to ride out, would not remain a party of four all through. 'If Lazarus does come in, starts asking questions, you can say we were here, an' where we were when you saw us last. If you don't somebody else will. If nobody here goads Arn, he'll ride on. This place is too big for him to do anything else. Right now, I've got to see to our horses, make sure they're all sound an' ready to go.' Quinlan left him. His attitude towards Olman was by no means an accurate reflection of his present feelings. Quinlan was in fact concerned that they spend no more time in this town than was absolutely necessary. The thought that Lazarus, having not only discovered that Cull was already dead, but maybe that there was a young daughter who had been spirited away, was haunting Quinlan, knowing that, Alys having already demonstrated that she was not a particularly confident rider, the gap between his party and the probable pursuers could be shortening by the hour.

★ ★ ★

They had come hammering into Abbott's Forge, Arn Lazarus in the lead, the other three bunched up, fifty yards behind. In rising clouds of dust they came reining in, head-tossing

134

horses blowing and screwing around, side-stepping, outside the mercantile. Lazarus's death-pale eyes raked up and down the main street that was swiftly being vacated by all who were close enough to get a good look at these men who had arrived so suddenly.

For a short time they sat their saddles, then Phelps dismounted and tossed the reins of the horse to Asa Lodd. Phelps unslung saddlebags and walked dustily inside the mercantile, giving the door a rattling kick on the way in to wake up those inside.

Those outside now went bobbing along Main, Lodd leading Phelps's sweating animal, towards a black and white sign that said Ace Livery and Corral. Here, all three swung down and began yelling for the liveryman. A very fat individual took a look outside and would have withdrawn had not Jack Guido, thongs hanging loose either side of his dust-caked, dark, unshaven face, gone striding in.

'Git these here hosses cooled an'

fed an' watered. We'll be back in an hour.' He did not wait for an answer, but, quite confident that what he had instructed would be done, took a pace or two away, leaving, until Lazarus, outside, said something, and Guido turned and came back. He questioned the liveryman about other travellers through Abbott's Forge in recent times, specifically a girl and three men who had, in all probability, been heading north. When the round-bodied liveryman, who was of no great intellect, was slow in answering, Guido drew a long pistol and cocked it and shoved the barrel deep into the man's yielding belly.

'Five Goddamn' seconds, mister, startin' from now.'

The liveryman was able to give immediate confirmation. Yes, there had been such a bunch of people.

'How far ahead?'

''Bout a day, mister.' Guido swore and lifted the pistol until its ugly black eye was all but touching the liveryman's wet lower lip. The man said, 'They come in fer a pack-animal they'd left here, that's all . . . ! Four, there was then, headin' south. No girl. This time, her an' three men, headin' north.'

Narrow-eyed, Guido took this in. One man short, coming back out. They must have lost one to Dave Cull. That old Mex whore had kept saying there was one dead, besides Cull. It stacked up, anyway, with the three fresh graves at that farm, two of them close together, the other several yards away from them.

'North, you're tellin' me. That's fer certain?'

'Rid out that end o' Main, there, an' kept right on goin'; three men, the girl — not much more'n a kid — an' one pack-horse.'

Guido uncocked the big pistol, slid it back in its holster and went tramping out.

From there, afoot, spurs clinking, they all walked around to a clapped-out saloon at which they sat drinking for half an hour or more. The few other customers soon went quietly drifting away. A lone bar-dog was moving carefully up and down behind his long bar, watching the drinkers but contriving not to engage any eye. From deeply shadowed doorways the drinkers were being covertly examined, too, by the proprietor here, his middle-aged wife and daughter, a sallow woman of perhaps twenty. One good look at Lazarus and his companions was enough. The saloon-keeper made silent, insistent signals to his womenfolk to get the hell out of sight and stay there and stay quiet until these men had left. The two women went, whispering, away. The saloon-keeper, relieved, turned around to find Asa Lodd was right there, pistol in hand, his yellowed teeth prominent.

'Knowed there'd be whores in a dump like this,' Asa said, and called over his shoulder, 'They're sure 'nough back here Arn! Two on 'em!'

The proprietor, a balding man about

half Asa's height, started protesting that the only women back here were his own wife and daughter, nobody else, and that he would swear to. He had just finished saying this when Lodd split open the man's bare scalp with the barrel of the pistol, pounding the man to the floor.

To the bar-dog, Jack Guido said, 'I'd take a shot or two m'self, was I you, an' keep your long beak in back o' that there bar.'

Lazarus and Guido joined Lodd just as Joshua Phelps came in. 'Reckoned to find yuh here.' He threw what clearly were more heavily packed saddlebags across one of the round, stained tables, and came to where his companions were disappearing into the farther reaches of the building.

The women had run, of course, but they were caught not far from the top of the back stairs.

★ ★ ★

Alys, whether on her own initiative or having been guided by Belle, had been fitted out with clothing more appropriate for riding than that which she had worn and brought with her when coming from the farm. By the time they left Dolomite she had been clad in a blue and white checkered shirt and a tan-coloured, divided skirt, and a suitable wide-brimmed hat; and on her very slim hands were soft leather gloves. She was still riding the horse that had been Macafee's, a new bedroll secured behind the cantle. This horse of Macafee's, an animal which, in the past, had not been noted for good temper, seemed to have accepted its new, lightweight rider with remarkable equanimity.

No such affinity was evident, however, between Belle and Alys. If there had been a brief coming together over the matter of purchasing clothes, it had not been sufficient to breach the invisible barrier which (on Belle's part, anyway) had come up between them, early-on. Which, of course, had had much to do with the apparent understanding that had sprung up between Quinlan and Dave Cull's daughter; seemingly effortless, anticipatory. As far as Belle was concerned, however, it was like a burr under the saddle, and the atmosphere which now prevailed among the group that was now well on the way along the trail, meant that for the most part they were riding in silence.

For Bishop, this lack of conversation was not unwelcome, his mind now being heavily engaged by concerns over their relatively slow progress. The somewhat somnolent pack-animals were not helping, nor was the fact that the girl, Alys, was not a practised rider. Allowances were having to be made, not least for the fact that Quinlan, apparently sensitive to the girl's wariness of the big horse under her, had called for more rests than ordinarily he would have done.

To have time to himself, to think,

Bishop had been trailing for a little while, leading one of the pack-horses, but now increased his pace until he came level with Quinlan who was leading the other pack-animal. 'Need to push it along some, Tom. If the bastard's comin', he'll be comin' fast.'

Quinlan looked at him soberly. It was unlike Bishop to reveal anxiety in this way. Naylor would have thought nothing of it, but it was by no means Bishop's style.

They were watching the women bobbing along ahead of them, Belle out front, then fifteen yards behind her, Alys, her dark hair, tied with a scrap of blue ribbon at the neck, cascading down her narrow back like shiny pitch.

Quinlan said, 'A few more miles on, this side of Mendel, that's where we'll leave you. Once we've gone, you can push on faster.'

Bishop looked across to their right, contemplating the heat-misted, rising, broken, ugly country lying in that direction, rocky ravines, steep pine-slopes, difficult going, as he knew, some places that were full of slab-rock and sliding faces of scree. It spread over a big area, heat trapped in oven-like fissures just wide enough to admit horse and rider. But at a certain point in this traverse that Quinlan intended doing, there could be gained a high plain almost enclosed by rocky peaks and through which cut the Loesser River, at this time often a sorry waterway, but a lethal torrent during the snow-fed spring.

When they next drew rein it was at the place that Quinlan had chosen to depart from Bishop and Belle. They all got down and stretched cramped limbs, Alys sinking down to sit on the ground. To Quinlan, standing a little apart still, Bishop said, 'That sure is bad country, Tom. Went in there myself, once, years back.' He did not say why. 'Naylor, he knew it a lot better than me, but he didn't fancy it neither.' It must have been on some bounty hunt. And

Naylor's negative opinion came as no surprise. Bishop now advanced another and unappealing possibility. 'If it all turns to shit, if Arn cottons on to where you've taken her, what'll you do? I mean, before you get through, towards Morwenna? She's no rider. He could run you down.'

Quinlan confessed that he had no detailed plan, but with a small stick drew marks on the dirt, quietly putting forward what he admitted was something of a last resort option. Bishop studied it sombrely. Finally he said, 'Christ, Tom, you'd best hope they don't get you boxed in a place like that.' He went to his saddlebags, withdrew the spyglass and handed it to Quinlan. 'You might need it more than me.' It was an act which was to have some bearing on what happened.

★ ★ ★

After the wild riders had gone hammering out of Abbott's Forge, a

144

bar-dog had come edging out through the batwings of the saloon, looking up and down the quiet street and calling for assistance. His employer was still lying in a pool of his own blood and was not responding to shaking and questioning. And there were two very distressed women in the place, their clothing almost all torn from them, bruised, sobbing and wailing. Arn Lazarus. Something to remember him by.

Now they were on the trail again, Lazarus once more leading out. The short spell in Abbott's Forge and the bonus taken there had been well enough, but all that would be as nothing, Lazarus had assured them, once they caught up with and took Dave Cull's little whelp. The question now was whether or not to pass through the large town of Dolomite or pass it by. Maybe Asa Lodd could go in and take a look, just to make sure Quinlan was not holed up there somewhere, and pick up any word that could be got.

But Lazarus did not really expect to find Quinlan or any of his party in Dolomite. They had taken the girl with them for a very good reason. She was a Cull. They were getting her out of the way of Arn Lazarus. Well, the bastards had best think again.

10

Bishop and Belle were making better time but were still not moving as quickly as Bishop would have liked, for the trail was not a good one around here. They were a few miles out of Mendel, the small, dirty, forgettable place that they had been pleased to see fall behind them. Bishop was leading the pack-horse and was sparing no effort to make sure it was kept coming along steadily. Belle was feeling uncomfortable in the heat, and showing it, but was none the less determined that she would not display any real weakness to Bishop, believing that if she did, at some later time an opinion of it would be relayed to Quinlan.

Quinlan was much in her thoughts, and so, indeed, was Alys Cull, a startlingly lovely, if impaired young creature who had come out of nowhere. Maybe these recurring thoughts led her into inattention, for when what was maybe only a shadow from a quickly moving cloud caused the horse under her to take momentary but violent fright, she did not handle the abrupt movement well, and before she realized what was happening, the animal kneed down and Belle herself went tumbling over its head. She struck the ground heavily and went rolling dustily, arms and legs flailing. It happened so fast, however, that her body had not had time to tense up, so that she hit the ground slackly, yieldingly, suffering only a few bruises and no broken bones.

Alarmed, Bishop brought his animals to a halt and, swinging down, came hurrying to her. 'By God . . . ! Belle . . . !'

'It's all right Bish . . . I'm all right. Oh, look! The horse . . . !'

Indeed the horse was in dire trouble,

screaming and trying to get up, one foreleg snapped.

'No good, Belle,' Bishop said. 'Got to finish him.' Already he was unscabbarding his rifle. The lash of the shot assaulted her eardrums as she sat on the ground, her arms now wrapped around her head. 'Oh, God, Bish . . . I'm so sorry . . . ! It wasn't his fault. It was mine.'

Bishop knelt down and took her in a surprisingly gentle fashion by the upper arms. 'Don't take it hard. Happens to plenty of riders. Just so long as you're not hurt bad.'

'It jarred every bone I've got . . . but no, I'm all right.'

'Here . . . Best you stand up and walk around.' He gripped one of her gloved hands and helped her to her feet. Gasping, and at first unsteady, Belle tested her legs, then pressed her fingers to the small of her back and walked around slowly.

'I'm still not sure what went wrong, Bish.'

'Coulda been anything. Shadow, small animal. Seen 'em spooked by less.'

She said, 'What happens now?'

Bishop stood rubbing slowly at his jaw. 'One option's heading on back to Mendel. If there's a horse worth callin' a horse to be had there, I could fetch it here.' Though he had said it, she could tell that he did not fancy the idea at all. 'The other is dump some of your stuff an' put your saddle on the pack-horse.' She must have looked dubious because he said then, looking back down the trail. 'If old Naylor was here, he'd say this was a bad omen. For once, I mightn't argue.'

'You really believe they might be that close behind?'

Bishop shrugged. 'It's possible. C'mon, I'll haul the saddle off this poor ol' feller. Start dumping the stuff off the other.' As far as Bishop was concerned, the slow progress to the point at which Quinlan and Alys had split away, and a less-than-hoped-for increase in pace thereafter, had altered the entire face of this business. At the outset, Tom Quinlan had been confident that Bishop and Belle would be able to get far enough ahead to put themselves well beyond any possible threat from Arn Lazarus. Now, as then, Bishop was far from certain about that, and could not have concealed from the woman — even had he wished to do so — that he was more often inclined to turn to stare back the way they had come. And now they would be leaving behind them a marker; the dead horse and some jettisoned belongings. Bishop had a feeling that the entire enterprise had started to unravel.

★ ★ ★

Quinlan, already dismounted, helped her down. Light as a wind-blown leaf, she was. He stepped away, and, tired though she must be, and uncomfortable in the relentless, enclosed heat, she gave him a wide smile.

'A half hour here is all,' Quinlan told her, thinking it best not to mislead her into believing that the day's riding was over. If she was disappointed, she did not show it, merely nodded and reached to unsling her canteen. When she had taken a small drink, however, she pulled a face, restoppered the canteen and returned it to its place on the horse.

Quinlan pointed to the way ahead. At present they were in an area of stony ground between two great upthrusts of rock. Behind them lay the tough, piney slope that had tested the horses, and ahead of this comparatively level shelf lay a rock-toothed ravine which, in some places, was almost choked with brush; but this would lead to an elevated ledge among slab-rock and stunted pines and, as Quinlan now indicated by pointing and saying, 'Once up there, we should come to a place where there's water,' Perhaps a hint that they would make a camp. Indeed, if his recollection was correct, there ought to be a random tributary of the upper Loesser River flowing down from the heights that, from where they stood, were painted dizzyingly against the sky. This entire area of split and ravaged country looked as though at some time far in the past, some massive upheaval had occurred, and this jumble of rock and ravines and uncertain footing where only hardy pines and brush had found nurture, had been the outcome.

Alys moved across to a wedge of shade cast by one of the granite upthrusts. She undid two buttons of her checkered shirt, pulled the bottom of the garment loose from the waistband of her riding skirt and stood flapping the shirt in an effort to cool her body. It was probably having little effect, Quinlan thought.

Quinlan turned away and fetched Bishop's spyglass from a saddlebag, then slipped the blue bandanna from his neck. This he wrapped around the extended spyglass in the hope that by so doing the risk of sunflash off the brass would be reduced. He then went pacing to where he could look back into the heat-shimmering distance of their sloping back-trail, or as much of it as was visible. Quinlan was seeking evidence of any rising dust that could mean the presence of horsemen. Nothing. For the present. Unwrapping the spyglass he came back to where Alys was, and to her lifted brows, shook his head. Then he repeated what he had said earlier about the possibility of fresh water and, 'Sooner we get on up there, the sooner we'll find it.' In her expression there was no evidence of any demur. They went across to the horses and Quinlan gave her a boost up into the saddle and saw the white flash of her teeth as she grimaced at the sudden sear of the hot leather.

Quinlan had to lead off again, trailing the nodding pack-horse, Alys some ten yards behind that animal, sitting with her small body hunched slightly forward as though she was in fear of sliding from the big horse's back. She must often have noticed the hard, dark-moustached face turned to look back at her. Once, he said, 'Relax. Ride easy. You tense up an' he'll feel it an' he'll not go well for you.' The next time he took a look she was sitting more loosely, seeming more confident. 'That's it. That's well done,' he called, and she flashed him one of her flawless smiles.

So they continued their sweating, plodding ascent, winding in among rocks and brush, weather-smoothed stones sometimes sliding beneath the feet of the horses. Quinlan was impelled to keep turning to look at her, knowing that should some mishap occur she could not alert him by calling. Her heart-shaped face, like his own ravaged one, was plastered with dust and runnelled with sweat and her mouth was set firm; yet every time he glanced back, she smiled at him. At each of the brief rests he had permitted since departing from the Dolomite-Mendel trail, heading up into this very rough country, the understanding between them had developed further. A touch, a gesture, a nod, a lift of eyebrows: '*I see.*' '*I understand.*' '*Do you follow what I mean?*' '*Do you wish me to write?*' (She had brought a supply of paper and a pencil and she carried the pencil and one sheet of paper in a shirt-pocket.) No trace of reticence or embarrassment. A special, soft, fleeting touch of silk-soft fingers. '*I knew you would understand.*' And: '*Will you give me time to myself?*' Indeed, Quinlan in his time had encountered plenty of people much less articulate than Alys Cull. Yet physically she did not look strong, and as this day wore on it would not surprise him too much if, at one of their pauses to rest, she was unable to face yet another wearing stint in the saddle.

★ ★ ★

Belle, though she had been determined to tough out the remainder of the ride to Carver, had had to admit that she was badly shaken and needed to wait for a while before remounting and going on.

'I'm sorry, Bish, truly I am.'

Again he told her, 'It happens to a lot of riders.'

The horse that had been laden with belongings and food and extra water now stood ready for her, saddled, laden only with the extra water and saddlebags containing mainly food.

'I'll be all right soon,' she told him.

'Take your time,' Bishop said. He sounded relaxed, reassuring, but behind the mask he must have felt mounting anxiety. By this time Quinlan and Alys Cull would be somewhere on the lower slopes of that tough country they had set out to cross, and with any luck would have thrown any pursuers off the scent. Of Lazarus, Bishop himself had said to Quinlan, 'If the bastard's comin', he'll be comin' fast.'

Suddenly Belle asked, 'What possessed

him to do it, Bish? Bring her out of there?'

'What Dave said to him, how he said it, far as I can tell.'

She badly wanted to ask 'If she'd been stoop-shouldered, plain as a dishcloth and smelled, do you think he'd still have done it?' But she drew back from exposing that side of her mind, from confirming what Bishop might have already suspected. Instead, she said, 'I made a bad mistake. I should never have come. I should have kept well clear, just waited for you all to come back. Naylor sure thought so, and I see that he was right.'

Slightly uncomfortable with the turn the conversation had taken, Bishop said, 'Naylor. Ol' dog-face. Well I've never known him to be content, no matter what.'

She had been half lying on the ground but now she struggled to her feet. 'It's past time we were on our way. I've held us back long enough.'

They remounted and headed away.

A mile further on Bishop held up a gloved hand and they drew rein. Bishop swung down and handing the reins of his horse to Belle, made his way up an incline to the left of the trail, there to take yet another long look back the way they had come.

* * *

Arn Lazarus, boots set apart, arms folded, stood staring back down the trail that had brought them into the town of Mendel. Dusty, with red-rimmed eyes, Jack Guido came scuffing to him.

'Back there somewheres,' Lazarus said. 'Back there somewheres the bastard cut away. Four rid out o' Dolomite, two men, two women. Two come through this dump, one man, one woman. Not a girl, a woman.' For he had done his hard asking and had received instant answers.

Guido said, 'I'll go git Josh an' Asa. We'll head on back.'

Lazarus, his pale eyes lit with an odd fire, now stood punching one gloved hand into the palm of the other. When Guido turned to go, Lazarus said, 'Wait, Jack.'

Guido stopped. 'Yuh still want that li'l Cull, we got to go back.'

'An' start lookin' where?' Lazarus turned his death-eyes on Guido. 'The two that come through here, they can't be far. Two of 'em, one of 'em a woman, an' a pack-animal. I git to them, they kin tell me where Quinlan's gone.' He showed his stained teeth. 'The lady'll tell me. She'll be quicker'n that ol' greaser whore was.'

Asa Lodd came bumbling out of a saloon, a bottle in one hand, and stood on the boardwalk pissing into the street. Guido yelled, 'Go git Josh! We're headin' out!'

Lazarus went striding away to his tied horse. By the time the others were mounted he was a good hundred yards out of Mendel, going at a dead run, intent on coming up with the man and woman who were said to be heading north from Mendel.

* * *

Quinlan walked his horse into a level clearing among battlements of baking rock, and Alys, moving up alongside him, glanced across and made a little, graceful flowing motion with a hand, gentle as a fluttering butterfly, and cupped her other hand to an ear. Quinlan had not yet heard anything, but sure enough, as they crossed to the other side of this open place and passed among other large rocks, he heard the stream running, then caught sight of the glitter of the water, between clumps of brush.

Quinlan stopped. So did Alys. Quinlan said, 'Well, now we know where the water is. Cold, too, no doubt, coming down over stones from the higher country up there.'

Alys pointed. There, some fifty feet below, down a steep, brushy slope and half in shadow, was a glassy rock-pool, the overflow from it doubtless cascading down a further slope. Quinlan made a hand motion. 'We'll go on back to that open place, make a camp there.'

A flicker of expression passed across her small face. Relief.

★ ★ ★

For the third time within an hour Bishop had Belle come to a stop while he went to higher ground from which to study their back-trail. It was not until beyond mid-afternoon, however, that he saw, or believed he saw, what he had not wanted to see.

Thankfully, Belle had dismounted and was standing at the heads of both horses, holding them. But she could tell now from the way Bishop was behaving that he thought he had seen something. At some distance, but there. Before looking again, he rubbed at closed eyelids. The woman was aching to call out and ask him what he could see, but as time had gone on and his anxiety had grown, she had discovered that it was not advisable to ask him questions until he was good and ready to give answers.

When he came down the slope — taking care not to break into a boot-sliding run — Belle could now see from his taut face that he was deeply concerned. Before she could ask, he said, 'There's some dust. Still a helluva long ways off. It's not just wind-rise. An' it's got to be more than one rider.'

'Do you think it's a chance that it's Lazarus?'

'It could be. It could be just some cowmen on the move, heading for Carver. But listen, Belle, this is the time we've got to face up to the big risk. So what you have to do is get on this horse of mine an' go full out for Carver. Now. Run him 'til he has to blow, give him some time to come back to it, then run him again.'

163

'Both of us have to go.'

Bishop shook his head. 'This other feller, he's not up to a run like that. He'd probably drop dead. No, you go, Belle, on the other. Even after sundown, don't stop. Check him back, but don't stop.'

'What about you?'

'I'll get me a closer look at 'em, whoever they are. I'll take good care.' Hurriedly he began unloading his gear from the horse she was to ride, leaving her the canteen.

'And you'll follow as soon as you can?'

'I will.' He added the unlikely opinion, 'I'll be but a couple of hours behind you. Go on Belle.'

'But if it does turn out that it's . . . '

'Go, Belle.' She did, with one agonized look at him, as though her thoughts, no matter what he had said, had gone down another dreadful path, in tandem with his own.

Bishop led the remaining animal off the trail and in among boulders and brush, then went back and collected his belongings. He slipped his rifle from the scabbard and prepared to wait. He would have given a lot to have still had the spyglass.

11

Quinlan must have appeared anxious but Alys grinned and made signs which plainly said that she would be perfectly safe. But he said, 'Take it careful, Alys. Some of the rock hereabouts could be rotten.'

She nodded, but down she went, confidently finding firm footing and hand-balances. He was not satisfied, however, until he had watched her arrive safely on a broad shelf of rock which jutted out just above the water.

What happened next he was unprepared for. In shorter time than he would have believed possible, she was completely out of her clothing, boots, skirt, yellow and blue shirt and underwear, revealing a slim, dark-tressed, ivory figure swelling into early womanhood, a sight that caused him to catch his breath. Alys was perfectly aware that he was still there, above her, and glanced up, her white teeth flashing. And then she was gone, into the pool, a pale, smooth sliver of body, the clear water gulping her in, and he could see clearly her ripple-ribbed form lithely turning underwater, then sending bright, glass-like beads bursting as she came to the surface, rising swiftly up and out to the level of her flat belly, then rolling over, diving deep again. When she came up again, her long, dark hair plastered to her back and narrow shoulders, she beckoned to him, but Quinlan shook his head briefly and went tramping away.

At the chosen camp-site he attended to the horses, taking all the gear off and dumping it on the ground. He did not tie the animals for there was virtually nowhere they could go. Then he went fossicking around under scrappy brush, collecting sticks to make a fire; but he would not light it yet while the sky was still holding light, for he did not want to send up smoke that might be noticed, and from a considerable distance.

Something else that had happened during the late afternoon continued to haunt him. It had occurred during one of their short rests. Suddenly Alys had plucked at his sleeve and made her gesture for 'Listen . . . !' Faintly, but to Quinlan, when his own ear became attuned, unmistakable. Distant gunfire. Silently he had tapped the shiny stock of the scabbarded rifle. There was nothing to be said, nothing that could be done. But it was there, still, echoing in his mind, images accruing to it that he would rather have thrust out of sight.

The fire would be lit after sundown. This place was high enough and immediately secluded enough for a fire not to be seen except by somebody very close by, and as far as he had been able to determine, there was no-one. Just him and Alys Cull.

Almost thirty minutes went by before

she reappeared. Obviously she had sun-dried herself, or nearly so, though her hair was still slickly wet, and she had dressed. The first thing she did, however, was go to where her own belongings lay and he watched her fish out a clean shirt, a red and black checkered one, and her pale, narrow back, overlaid by her long hair, flashed whitely in the dying light as she took off the shirt she had redressed in, and slipped the other one on.

When she turned and saw him looking at her she came nearer, grinning, and the mime, tips of fingers to cheeks, then pointing to him, then herself, asking plainly, *'Have I embarrassed you?'*

Smiling slightly, Quinlan shook his head. 'You took me by surprise, is all.' Again she pointed to him, then in the direction of the pool. He said, 'You're damn right I am.' And, 'I'll leave you to get the food ready for cooking later. When I get back, I'll make a fire.' He went trudging off out of the camp-site,

heading to where he would climb down
to the rock-pool.

★ ★ ★

Bishop had given it plenty of thought
and had come to his decision. The
horse he had led in among some
aspens, and there had divested it of
saddle and all other gear. All his
belongings he had heaped near by.
Into every available pocket he had put
spare ammunition, and now, rifle in
hand, he was leaning against a smooth
grey boulder down nearer the trail,
watching the oncoming riders. Much
closer now, he believed that there
were four of them. Bishop's logic
was simple. If these people turned
out to be cowmen or any other
harmless travellers going about their
own affairs, then while there might
be some annoyance, no harm would
be done. If, on the other hand, this
was Arn Lazarus, with others, coming
after him and Belle, then Bishop had

made up his mind what he must do. If Lazarus were to be permitted to ride on by, unimpeded, there would be little doubt that he would run her down. Knowing the terrible reputation of the man, Bishop did not wish even to contemplate such an outcome.

The immediate area did offer some cover. There were numerous large boulders like this one, some green brush and a few clumps of trees. But the ground on either hand rose above the trail, the more so on the opposite side. Bishop was acutely aware that if anyone who wished to do him harm were to manage to get to some point that overlooked where he was, he would be presented with dire problems. First, he had considered occupying a higher position himself; but if this was Lazarus coming, then by the time Bishop had identified him it might well be impossible to prevent him passing.

So here Bishop was, almost on the trail itself, waiting. He wondered how far Belle had got. Turning his head, he could see that the whitish dust of her departure had dissipated. Again he looked to his front. By this time he could hear the approaching horses as well as see them, and by God, these men were wasting no time, one of them out front by some thirty yards, the others, three of them, in a bunch. Bishop straightened away from the boulder and walked slowly out onto the trail, holding the rifle across his body, a round already jacked into the chamber.

Sixty or seventy yards short of him the leading rider saw him and came hauling to a slithering halt, dust rising, the following horsemen likewise reining in, but by the time their mounts came to a head-tossing halt they were close up behind the man who had been leading them.

The first thing was that these men were not cowmen. The next was that Bishop could recognize the general set of the big man who had been out front even before Lazarus, his horse having screwed sideways, called, 'Reckoned we'd come up with yuh, by an' by, Bishop!'

The eyes of those behind Lazarus were probing left and right of the trail, clearly looking for horses and no doubt looking for the woman known to have been with Bishop when he had ridden out of Mendel. They would also be well aware of the rifle Bishop was holding. No-one made a move towards a rifle, and for pistol work the range was somewhat long for certainty. Bishop lifted his own rifle and held it butt-place to shoulder. 'Time to turn around, Arn. This way's blocked.'

Lazarus was staring fixedly at Bishop. 'That bein' the case, we'll have to see about gettin' it unblocked. Where's the woman?'

'Long gone,' Bishop said.

'Not so long gone, I'd say,' said Lazarus. 'Reckon I seen dust.' Then, 'It's Tom Quinlan I want.'

'No,' Bishop said, 'that's not true. It's Alys Cull you want.'

Lazarus said something to the men behind him, then all four turned their horses and headed back up the trail, Bishop tracking them with his rifle. Not until they were more than four hundred yards from him did he lower it. Bishop was under no misapprehension, though. They were not leaving, merely drawing back from the threat of Kel Bishop with a rifle in his hands.

Some of them, at least, would try to occupy higher ground, and from there pick him off with rifle fire. And they were a formidable bunch. Bishop had recognized Jack Guido and Asa Lodd and believed that the fourth man was a certain Joshua Phelps. Bishop's head lifted slightly. They were splitting up. Bishop went trotting past the rounded boulder where he had stood, earlier, and up a slight slope, among brush and towards the aspens where the horse was. But he was also doing his best to keep an eye on what they were up to. And what that was, was not long in taking shape.

They had dismounted and picketed their horses out of view. Now they were coming at him, afoot, carrying their own rifles and glimpsed from time to time slipping from cover to cover, boulders and brush, two on Bishop's side of the trail, two on the other.

It was not long before one of them shot at him, but obviously on the fly, for the bullet came nowhere near him. He was not drawn into a reply, which might have given away too soon his own position. All had fallen quiet and time went sliding by. They seemed to have gone to ground. Bishop stayed still, doing his best to see between spiky branches of brush, listening for any evidence of anybody on the move. More time passed by. Nothing. Bishop glanced at the sky. Bright fire was flaring in the west. Maybe sundown was what they were waiting for. Suddenly another thought came to him and he sank down gently to rest on one knee, bringing the rifle around, then pulled the brim of his hat further down, squinting into the long, bright fingers of the lowering sun. One or more of them would come out of that. And, by God, there was one of them now. Bishop knew he had been too slow. Even as his eye caught the slight flick of movement, a rifle shot lashed and Bishop was hit.

It felt like a whack with a hot iron, the bullet tearing through his left rib-cage, knocking him to the ground. Bishop's head was roaring, the real pain after the shock of the bullet-strike not yet begun. The rifle had fallen and he was groping for it. Dimly he was aware of shouting and now had the impression of boots running. Sweat slicking over face and body and his shirt sodden with blood, Bishop, blood also on his left hand, was somehow managing to get the rifle up, and pretty much on instinct almost at once got his target. It was Joshua Phelps who had shot him and was now coming in too quickly, lacking proper caution. Bishop, on hands and knees, shot Phelps and killed him instantly, blowing .44 calibre lead through the man's right eye, red spray leaping from the back of Phelps's head, and with it, brain matter and fragments of bone.

Bishop went crawling away, badly hurt, seeking better cover, and managed to get himself in behind a clay bank, and once there, jacked a round into the chamber, though now both of his hands were slippery with blood. Voices were yapping, like a pack of dogs scenting a kill, even after what had happened to Phelps. Bishop, making a strong effort, struggled to move his position. He was in serious pain now, the lump of lead still inside him. Somewhere over to his left and down on the level ground where the trail was, there was some movement. At once Bishop shot at it. He did not think he had hit anybody, but after that one echoing shot all fell quiet again. Bishop wiped his face and neck with his bandanna, then dragged out his watch and tried to focus on it, then put it away. Every minute that went by meant that Belle was further away from here, from Lazarus.

They must have pinpointed where he was, for there erupted more gunfire, the beginning of a sustained attack, from a distance, the sounds of the rifles like the cracking of a dozen bullwhips, lead humming over his head and slashing through nearby brush and howling off rocks. Then the gunfire stopped and the silence ran on, as though the shooters were waiting for a reaction. Bishop did not move. But he was well aware that soon his strength must begin ebbing away. Stiffly and painfully he removed the bandanna, formed it into a rough pad and pushed it inside his shirt, over the nasty wound, and almost cried out in agony. Then he thought how absurd this act had been. Surely there must soon be an onslaught; but time went ticking on and it did not come. The sun had now passed below the hills and the light was a soft greyness, not yet night, but less than daylight.

Bishop set the butt-plate of the rifle on the ground and, using the weapon as a support, struggled to his feet, then stood breathing hard, sweating profusely. He took the rifle in both hands and stood swaying, listening. Still the strange silence went running on. But then, quite suddenly, there they were.

The first one he saw was Jack Guido, below and to the left, making an attempt to further outflank him. Bishop shot at Guido but missed. The grey shadows were lengthening, the light finally failing. Bishop took a pace forward, then another. Now he could see all three of them, and as he shot and laboriously levered and shot again, their lead came whanging in, one bullet breathing past Bishop's face as he came out at them.

Twenty paces separated each of them. All had rifles levelled as Bishop came on, snarling like some wounded, maddened grizzly, set to tear the heart out of his tormentors. Bishop was shooting, levering and shooting again as he came, his eyes refusing to focus now, walking his last walk, taking the hits, beyond true awareness, not realizing that, punched hard, his body had been turned by the impact of lead, that his left elbow had been blown away, that his belly was punctured, his intestines about to come oozing from the hole. Then the top of his head was blown away. He had got to within forty feet of them, had failed to hit any of them; but he had bought Belle very nearly an hour on her flight to Carver, and safety.

12

Alys had wrapped herself in an extra blanket and was lying as close to the fire as she could safely get, for the night was chill. Above them the sky was cloudless and filled with icy fires, but with only a pale reap-hook of a moon. Quinlan threw more brush on the fire, sending sparks spiralling upwards, new, dancing light reaching out.

It was then that he noticed that all was not well with the girl, her small form shuddering, and he heard the gasp that told him it was because she was sobbing. Quinlan turned from settling down on his own bedroll and went to her, bending closely over her.

'Alys?' No response. Clearly she was in some deep distress. It was unusual, too, that she was not acknowledging him, though she must have heard him plainly enough. One of his big hands he laid on a sharp, narrow shoulder. The touch was enough. Slowly, gropingly, she struggled to a sitting position, but would not look at him. Quinlan eased himself down alongside her, one of his arms encircling her. 'Alys? What is it? Is it about your ma?' For the space of several seconds there came no response whatsoever, then she nodded, and at almost the same instant turned her face to him, pressing in hard against his chest, Quinlan, without much choice, simply holding her firmly, aware of the warm, quivering life in her, even in her grief. Thus they remained for what must have been close to ten minutes, so long, in fact, that he thought, after her sobbing had ceased, that she must have fallen asleep. It was only then, as she withdrew and sat gently away, that he came to the realization that he had been rubbing softly at her back, as a parent might comfort a very young child. 'You all right now, Alys?' A jerky nod or two, and even the small beginnings of a smile. What had occurred must have come upon her in a sudden wave in the quiet night after all the tensions of a most difficult journey here, and the realization that with the exception of Hattie Nelson, in Morwenna, she was virtually alone in the world. Without speech. 'You'll sleep now?'

In the waving firelight he saw her nod again. But she also made small signs to him. He went to his bedroll and brought it closer, and dragged in the saddle to pillow his head. As he lay down under his blanket Alys rolled on her side and lay tucked into him, within his encircling arm. After all that she had gone through, he was surprised that she had managed to keep her sanity.

* * *

Without having held out much hope that it would bring a result in a town as substantial as Carver, Belle had made enquiries about Naylor. She

183

was astonished, therefore, when an old teamster who happened to overhear when she asked the question in a mercantile, touched his terrible hat and said that Naylor was indeed in town. So she found him, in the clanging, smoky yard of a smith, Naylor watching on sulkily while his horse was being reshod. When he turned his long face and saw Belle standing in the gateway, only a slight tightening of his mouth gave any indication that he was surprised to see her. Ordinarily, he was about the last man she would have sought out, but of course there was a lot of fear mixed up in it, over Bishop and about Tom Quinlan.

Naylor's hound-like face, as he came unhurriedly across the yard to her, revealed no warmth whatsoever, but there was obviously a certain curiosity. As soon as she set eyes on him she was assailed with a feeling of resentment that this man had lost no time at all in cutting free from Quinlan and

Bishop after the Cull business was over. Naylor asked, 'Where are they?' Not, '*You look real bad. What the hell's happened*?' And even to the most casual observer she must have looked to be in bad shape, moving very slowly and stiffly, her clothing covered in dust and with small rips in it.

'Tom's gone with Alys Cull, to Morwenna. Up through the Loesser country. I was on the way here with Kel Bishop . . . ' Belle, one of her rather dirty hands to her forehead, was suddenly overcome with dizziness, and if Naylor had not stepped forward quickly, she would have fallen on her face.

It was some time before Belle opened her eyes. No longer in the smith's yard, she was lying on a clean cot in a cream-painted, panelled room that reeked of numerous medicinal potions. A thin man with white hair, a pinkish scalp showing through, and with a white goatee, was looking down at her.

'Mrs Howell?' As her eyes focused on him, he said, 'Mrs Howell, I'm Doctor Genet.'

'What happened to me?' Surely it was not her own voice .

'You collapsed, lost consciousness. Not so surprising, by the looks of things.'

She was trying to sit up but Genet raised an admonitory finger. Belle said, 'I must talk with Mr Naylor. Where is he?'

'Mr Naylor brought you here. He's in my waiting-room. Mrs Howell, talking with Mr Naylor or anybody else must come later. At present you are in no fit state . . . '

'Please! I really do have to talk with him.'

Genet looked somewhat miffed at being resisted, his cheeks now as pink as his scalp, but he relented and allowed Naylor to come in, while the doctor himself, for the time being ('*Five minutes*') withdrew.

Naylor, a stony expression on his

186

face, heard her out. She repeated, 'Kel told me he'd be about two hours behind me.' When she said it aloud, it occurred to her just how naïve she sounded. If Naylor thought so too, perhaps in deference to the state she was in, he forebore to lay tongue to it. She asked, suddenly, 'How long have I been here?'

'Long enough,' Naylor said obtusely. To him, this in all likelihood was the ultimate outcome for an enterprise that he believed had been blighted from the beginning, and much of that had had to do with this woman lying on the cot.

As though clinging tenuously to hope, she asked, 'Will you go out and watch for Kel, and when he comes, tell him where I am?'

Naylor, standing there, holding his old hat, simply stared at her. Did she not realize that, if it had been Arn Lazarus approaching, Bishop would likely never be coming?

* * *

Lazarus and Asa Lodd were standing with their horses, having spent some time quartering the ground thereabout assiduously. Jack Guido, however, was still some hundred and fifty yards from them, down out of the saddle, leading his horse and staring at the ground, walking on, pausing, walking on again. After some quarter of an hour and now near to two hundred yards away, Guido looked towards them and raised his arm. Lazarus short-punched Lodd on the arm to wake him up. 'Looks like Jack's got a sniff.' They mounted their sweat-rimed horses and went bobbing away towards Guido.

As soon as they reached him, Lazarus swung down. Guido pointed with the toe of a boot. 'Ground's packed hard hereabouts, but them's tracks.'

Lazarus studied the faint marks. These tracks, such as they were, suggested that the horses that had made them were moving at right-angles to the Dolomite-Mendel trail. Lazarus lifted his eyes to the rise of the high, harsh country lying in that direction. It did not seem to make sense to Lazarus. Why would Quinlan take the girl into such a place? Guido and Lodd were looking at him, waiting for him to say what was to happen now.

★ ★ ★

Quinlan, lying with the bandanna-wrapped spyglass, shifted his position slightly for greater comfort, and concentrated. Eighty feet back of him, with the horses, Alys stood watching him. Quinlan's view was down a rocky slope and beyond that across treetops to other time-ravaged slopes and clumps of wind-warped pines. Whatever was moving, 'way down there was a hell of a long way off, and even through the spyglass, no more than juddering, smudgy specks. On forearms and knees, Quinlan came crabbing backwards away from the small lip of ground where he had been lying. Then, rising, but only to a crouch, he came back to Alys. The question was there, in her anxious face.

'Somebody,' Quinlan said. 'More'n one, but too far to get a look at. We'd best move on quick as we can. Now, listen to me, Alys. The way things are, we might not be able to get clear of this country before they get a lot closer to us. I reckon nobody but Arn Lazarus would want to come in here. But even if we should get down an' onto the Loesser Flats ahead of him, we'd have a feather of dust pointing to us all the way to Morwenna. We'd have to cut the pack-animal loose an' go all out for Morwenna. I doubt we'd make it. They've been smarter than I'd thought possible.' He saw no point in trying to put a better face on it. She was listening with rapt attention, nodding from time to time. ('*I understand, Tom.*')

'So, since I decided to come up

through here, I've had a scheme up my sleeve in case, somehow, they cottoned on to where we'd gone. We have to push on for another couple of miles, then climb onto a high plain; but instead of crossing it, eastward, we cut back an' follow the Loesser, upstream. It won't be easy going. In fact, Alys, it's damn' dangerous. But I reckon we can do it. We can hole up in what was a small town, a mining town, called Deadman's. Ghost town, it is. But before we go there, there's a place that overlooks the plain, so if they do come up, we should be able to see which direction they take. My bet is they'll ride east, the way they'd expect us to go. So then we go up to Deadman's, wait there a few days, a week maybe. No fires, so no coffee, no hot food. We'll have to get by on the cans of stuff we've got.'

She smiled, nodding again, and the butterfly gestures said, '*Wherever you say, I'll go.*' Today there had been no evidence of the grief she had given way to during the night. She had in fact slept deeply, even beyond the time when he had carefully disengaged himself, just before sunup, to go fill the canteens and get a makeshift breakfast ready.

Quinlan resisted the temptation to go back and take another look through the glass. An urgency to get on out of here was upon him. Once in here, they would surely come looking for all the traces, broken brush, horse apples, remnants of camps that it had been impossible to eradicate entirely. Somebody like Jack Guido whom he thought likely to be with Lazarus, could come sniffing along, more patient at that kind of work than Arn Lazarus. So once he and Alys gained the windswept plain, care would have to be taken to leave as few traces as possible. Quinlan moved his horse forward, towing the pack-animal, Alys following, handling Macafee's horse with more confidence as time went on, though having been sorely tested. Quinlan simply hoped that he had chosen the best option. It was her life he was gambling with and the knowledge chilled him. And once again the memory of distant rifle-fire came hauntingly back to him.

13

Two days had gone by since Quinlan
and Alys, lying in cover, exchanging the
spyglass, had watched three men, all
long-coated, riding slowly away in the
cold, whipping wind of that elevated
place, heading eastwards. Once, Lazarus
turning his head, Alys grimaced, seeing
that terrible face for the first time.

They were now in Deadman's. It
had not been easy getting there, at
one point having to pass along a ledge
no more than five feet in width, a wall
of black rock rising on one side and on
the other a steep drop of a hundred and
fifty feet into the Loesser River.

The long-abandoned town was a
bleak place, the more so because in
recent hours, clouds had come over,
very low, seemingly about to engulf
the derelict buildings themselves. The
horses had been taken to a patch of

bunch-grass growing inside the bounds of a building whose roof had long since vanished, perhaps plucked away in a gale. Quinlan had blocked off the two gaping doorways, using scraps of fallen lumber. The animals would be contained as well as being out of immediate view.

Few of the structures were of much use as shelters, but some had roofs that were at least partially intact. One of these had been a saloon (one of several in the town's heyday), another a large storehouse, a company building perhaps, and there were three others that had been ordinary dwellings. But the remainder of the town was a scattering of isolated walls, some of them stark false-frontages, and there were many small outbuildings in varying states of decay.

On the river side of the town, a trail had been hacked out of the rock, no doubt the work of a small army of men, so that access could be gained to the river itself; and all along the rocky edge of the water, numerous shacks had been constructed, but of these, only a few grey timbers remained.

Quinlan and Alys had stored their things in one of the old dwellings, one in which they had found the floor to be relatively sound. But they had not attempted to light the old iron stove. Two days had gone by, indeed, and they had begun to feel a small degree of security. 'But we have to be sure,' Quinlan said. 'Smoke might still be seen.' Alys made no argument. Only one suggestion had she resisted. He had assumed that she would occupy, on her own, one of two side-by-side rooms, but she had made signs that had left him in no doubt that she did not want to be separated from him. She had immediately confirmed it by placing her bedroll and other belongings alongside his own.

Now he came to the question of the route they would use to go to Morwenna, once Quinlan felt sure that it was safe for them to move out. In the damp-aired late afternoon, he said, 'As far as we know, they've crossed the plain an' by now they're down on the Loesser Flats. So right now they're between us an' Morwenna.'

Her hands and fingers asked, '*How will we get there?*'

'It might take longer than we'd thought.' He pointed in the direction she knew was upstream. 'Could be we'll need to go that way, try to get back down on the same side as the trail to Carver.' Full circle. When her delicate eyebrows lifted, 'Go the long way 'round. Touch Carver, then go in a wide loop, to Morwenna. Could take us more'n two weeks.'

Apparently not able to trust her signing to convey what she wanted to say, she took pencil and paper from her shirt-pocket, knelt on the floor and wrote. He bent his head to look. '*I have brought this on you. In Carver she will want you to stay with her. I must go on alone to Morwenna.*' And there was more to be read, but only in her face: sadness, but something resolute, too. It was still not easy for him to accept that this girl was Dave Cull's daughter. Whatever impulse moved him he did not know, but in the dying daylight he took her silk-soft face between his large hands. In this quiet place, all seemed remote. Carver. Morwenna. And people. Belle. It seemed an age since he had parted from her and Bishop.

'I'll not abandon you, Alys. I'll take you safe to Hattie Nelson. I *want* to do it.' And he would never know why he added, 'It's not all to do with . . . your pa.' Abruptly Quinlan turned away. After he had released her face she did not move for a little time but her fingers stole up to touch her own cheeks.

Quinlan went looking for a lamp that was still usable but failed to find one. When they settled for the night, not looking forward to the chill hours that yet must pass, in darkness, Alys, without artfulness wrapped herself in her blankets, then squirmed in under Quinlan's arm, burying her head like a sleeping cat.

On the fifth afternoon, which was somewhat brighter, Quinlan had not long come back from attending to the horses when Alys, in the act of opening a can of peaches, suddenly looked at him, her large, violet eyes widening, and now she was pressing a finger to her lips.

Quinlan had heard nothing but by now was well aware of the keenness of her hearing, and he stood still apart from a small movement of his head as he glanced at his rifle. His mouth formed 'What?'; she half turned to extend a hand, indicating the direction from which they had come into Deadman's.

Moving with caution, Quinlan crossed the room to pick up his rifle. Earlier he had cleaned and oiled the weapon and left it with a round in the chamber. Quietly he moved into the narrow hallway at the front of the house. Not quite emerging from the doorway he was able to get a view of the grass-thick thoroughfare that had been the main street.

Alys had remained where she was. Quinlan eased forward very slowly. In a breath of wind the long grass was moving slightly. All else stood silent, motionless. Quinlan withdrew inside the hallway. Alys came softly to him, touched one of her ears and nodded. (*'I did hear something'*) Quietly he said, 'I believe you.' They waited.

This time Quinlan heard it too. He moved to the doorway. Now there was something to see. About eighty yards away a lone horseman had arrived and drawn rein, glancing left and right as though taking merely idle interest in the scattering of ravaged structures of Deadman's. A man wearing a long, brown coat. As Quinlan looked on, another rider came walking his horse in, and some ten yards behind him another, both long-coated. They halted near the first one. Quinlan needed no spyglass to know that Arn Lazarus had arrived.

Alys had come to stand alongside him. Quinlan drew back, gently taking her with him. 'It's Lazarus.' The anguish on her face expressed all that Quinlan now felt. They had come all this way, taken many risks, done their utmost to stay one or two steps ahead of the man, had come to believe they had eluded him, and now here he was. Quinlan took another look. 'They're getting down.' One of them had taken charge of all three horses and led them to a warped tie-rail. The other two, one of them Lazarus, were walking around, looking here and there, seemingly unhurried, even casual. Quinlan, however, was not deceived. It was not in the nature of Arn Lazarus to be anything less than suspicious. For long enough his continued existence had depended on it. Quinlan murmured, 'There's no place to run, Alys. That has to be faced.' She was pale and very tense but there was no sign of outright panic. He turned from her to look again at what was happening along the street. But now all three men had vanished. So, too, had their horses. He told her, 'We'll have to stay right here. Just wait. You'll hear 'em before I do.' She managed a small, tight smile. It was not long before Quinlan's belief was borne out. Alys's fingers touched his arm and she indicated the opposite direction from where Lazarus had been seen. Somehow, without even Alys hearing anything, they had reached the other end of Deadman's. On an impulse, Quinlan led Alys through the house to the back door and opened it. There was no yard, as such, just more long grass and a few decrepit outbuildings.

Suddenly a pistol shot blasted. Then another. And another. Alys must have known even before Quinlan said, 'The horses. They've shot the horses.' Now Lazarus could come for them any time he wanted. The violet eyes of the girl searched the face of the dark-moustached man standing with her. They were three, these predators; he was but one. And now she and Quinlan had no means of getting out of this place, even if they could manage to elude the men who would be stalking them in earnest. All at once, from a little distance away, they heard a man's laughter. Quinlan said, 'Come on.'

They left the shelter of the house and went as quietly as they could through the long grass, away in the opposite direction, Quinlan anxious that they keep buildings or the remnants of buildings between themselves and Lazarus. But Alys's eyes were asking, *Where can we go?*

'At the far end, we can try to get across the street and climb down to the river. Maybe we can work our way along the edge, downstream. Soon, it'll be sundown.' Quinlan knew it was a flimsy scheme at best, but he had decided that it was better than getting trapped inside a tinder-dry structure and having Lazarus set fire to it. Far back, the way they had come, somebody called out, but not because they had been seen. It had been a muffled, indoors call, and meant, probably, that one of them had found Quinlan's and Alys's saddles and other things.

The rectangular, relatively sound building they had arrived at was the only saloon still standing. When Alys's movements asked, '*Do we go in here*?' he shook his head. 'Not an' risk having it burned around our ears.' Slim fingers crept to her lips. That had not occurred to her. With an arm across her shoulders Quinlan drew her around the corner of the saloon, while his eyes raked the surrounding grassy lots and tumbledown outbuildings. Now he disengaged from her. Grasping the rifle in both hands he took a cautious look back the way they had come.

And here, indeed, was one of them, a gangly man, his long coat open, pistol in hand, coming up the middle of the overgrown street at a long-striding walk. He saw Quinlan at the same instant that Quinlan saw him, and abruptly altered direction, and broke into a run. Before Quinlan could properly line him up, he had got in behind a warped, sagging frontage of what once had been a busy assay office. A door was hanging from one hinge, and to one side of that, a window in which half a pane of filthy glass had survived.

Asa Lodd, breathing hard, sure knew that he had been but a whisper away from taking a rifle bullet. He flattened himself inside the sagging frontage and tried to squint through the broken window of this place that stood anglewise across the street from where he had seen the dangerous Quinlan. Lodd had separated from Lazarus and Jack Guido, who were searching some houses near the one in which they had found Quinlan's saddles. But suddenly, there was Quinlan again.

Lodd extended his old, long, rakish pistol into the gap between frame and broken glass and fired, the pistol bucking and smoking. Just as quick as he had appeared, Quinlan had gone, but Lodd could not tell whether or not he had hit the bastard.

Quinlan had gone ducking away, giving Alys a push as he did so, .44 lead almost plucking at his bandanna. Whoever he was, Quinlan thought, he was good. In the glimpses that he had had, he would put money on it being a man named Asa Lodd. And at longish range, through the spyglass, up on the high plain, the other one riding with Lazarus was, confirming his earlier belief, Jack Guido. Something of a tracker, Guido. That would explain a lot. Quinlan knew that he had at least to move Lodd away before Lazarus and Guido arrived, circling, coming to the sounds of the shooting, to outflank him. The image of the broken window in his mind, Quinlan, rifle to shoulder, stepped quickly clear of the corner and let go a lashing shot. The dirty, broken pane was smashed again, and even as Quinlan went ducking back into cover, he could hear a man screaming, and when next he risked a look, saw Lodd come blundering out into full view, both of his hands up to his face, his head tilted down. The gangly man was swishing across the grassy street, animal noises coming from him, Lodd having been staring out, seeking a further sighting of Quinlan, when he sure got one, and when Quinlan's bullet shattered the glass, it had sent an arrowhead of it deep into Lodd's left eyeball.

Bright blood running between his fingers, Lodd was staggering, not going in a straight line, screaming again in agony. Quinlan came clear of the corner again, this time tracking Lodd with the rifle, squeezing a cracking shot away. Lodd's head snapped to one side, blood spraying as the .44 smashed his right cheekbone and exited through his left temple, the impact flinging Lodd into a wild, uncontrolled death-dance, to fall, then, among flower-headed weeds that were now spotted with the crimson of his lifeblood.

When the echoes of the rifle shot had gone slapping away to nothing among rock-faces, there fell an uncanny quiet. Quinlan knew that even now, Lazarus and Guido would be working their way round this saloon building, and spoke urgently to Alys. 'Cross the street, running. When I say, just go. I'll back across, to cover you. Get in behind the first cover you come to. *Now* . . . !'

Like a lithe young animal she went, dark hair streaming, every ounce of her trust placed in the big, moustached man to whom she had so quickly drawn so close. Quinlan, rifle reloaded and at the ready, came backing away, his eyes sweeping left and right, trying hopelessly to see all ways at once, stumbling in bunch-grass and weeds, recovering, until he felt her downy touch on his neck. Only then did he duck down, turn quickly and slip in behind a partly demolished store.

None too soon. One of them had come around the back of the saloon. Guido. Lazarus appeared almost at the same time, but further along the main street, evidence that they had thought to get him boxed between them. Lazarus, at least, must now be able to see exactly what had happened to Asa Lodd.

To Alys, Quinlan said, 'Hands an' knees. Crawl through the grass, that way, towards the river. Climb down out of sight. Work your way downstream.'

She went. He compelled himself not to watch her progress but concentrate on the movements of Guido and Lazarus. But he could hear the soft swishing of grass as Alys went crawling through it.

Guido had a pistol in hand, Lazarus carrying a rifle, and it was the rifle that was fired now, the bullet hammering into planks just above Quinlan's head. Guido was at the corner of the saloon where only a short time before, Quinlan and Alys had been. The air was very still. The light was draining from the day, but all could still be seen plainly.

Quinlan stepped clear of the sagging frontage, but was probably, because of the angle, not visible to Lazarus. Guido, though, saw him at once. Almost in unison Quinlan and Guido shot, the swarthy man's pistol bucking, and Quinlan felt a savage blow to his left side, at the hip, that sent him staggering, but Guido was also in trouble. Yet Guido, his shirt bloodied, was enraged, and with a huge effort of will, face contorted, eyes staring, came walking out onto the street, still somehow managing to shoot. The lead went humming by, but Quinlan's next rifle shot knocked Guido down as though he had been hit with an axe.

Quinlan was in pain, for Guido's bullet had clipped his left hip-bone, and now, sweating profusely, he had had to dive full length, rolling to lever the rifle as Lazarus, though some eighty feet away, having crossed the street, came striding between two ruined buildings, rifle at his shoulder. Quinlan, still shocked from the hit he had taken, was still struggling to get the rifle up. But he was at a dire disadvantage as Lazarus, his pale eyes without pity, came pacing forward, wanting to make quite certain of nailing him once and for all.

Lazarus fired, the lashing sound of the rifle seeming inordinately loud in Quinlan's ears and, surprised at not being hit even as he raised his own rifle, Quinlan saw that Lazarus had stopped abruptly, seeming to rise on the toes of his boot, and then, as a rifle was fired again, abruptly bent over, then fell to his knees, his head coming down.

Quinlan twisted painfully around. The man who was now behind Quinlan, who Lazarus had hit, but who had dropped Lazarus, was sitting in the long grass, also with his head down, his hat gone, his rifle lying near him. With difficulty, Quinlan rose and went to him and knelt down, putting his own rifle aside. Naylor's long dog-face lifted.

Naylor was dying, his lips bloodied, a hole punched in his chest, but he spoke audibly, if haltingly, first about Bishop and then about Belle. He had come in the first place to find out what had become of Bishop, and then by chance, had caught sight of Lazarus on his way into the Loesser country. Quinlan did not ask him what had moved him to follow Lazarus, who clearly was on Quinlan's trail. And Alys Cull's. Naylor would probably have declined to answer: Quinlan made as though to ease him down on his back but very slowly Naylor shook his head. Then he said, 'It was a Goddamn' heap o' shit from the start . . . ' And even as Quinlan watched, Naylor's eyes glazed over.

★ ★ ★

They had come to Morwenna, Quinlan and Alys Cull, Quinlan on the horse that had belonged to Arn Lazarus, Alys on Naylor's mount. And they had fetched in Jack Guido's and Asa

Lodd's horses as well. It had been a further day and a night before Quinlan was able to start the journey, and even then he had had to place much reliance on the young woman, whose confidence seemed to have been growing by the hour. Deeply shaken by events in Deadman's, Alys had none the less revealed an ability to keep her head.

She and Quinlan between them — albeit with difficulty — had dragged all of the dead inside the garbage-littered saloon. By the time they had ridden away and had come out onto the high plain, the climbing tower of smoke behind them had all but dissipated. For Quinlan, as a last act, and because he had no strength to bury them, had fired the building, creating a funeral pyre for four men, all that was left of Naylor being consumed along with the worldly remains of those same demons who had, from the outset of the Cull enterprise, haunted his back-trail.

Now, standing looking at the tall, elderly Morwenna doctor, Chaytor, the haggard Quinlan with his black-whiskered face and his red-rimmed eyes seemed capable only of repeating dully what Chaytor had just told them, as though to test the word for defects.

'Dead?'

'I'm afraid so,' said Chaytor, looking more often at Alys, now, than at Quinlan. 'About three months back. We had an outbreak, here, of some disease I still can't get a handle on. Some thought it was typhoid, but it sure wasn't. We lost seven people. All ages. One of them was Mrs Nelson. A great pity. A nice woman. A nice woman.'

So they went uncertainly away, Alys very downcast. Presently, Quinlan said, 'We'll rest up here a few days. Anyway, you might want to look through Hattie Nelson's things, if they're still around. (They were not. They had been burned on Chaytor's orders.) Then we'll go on to Carver.'

For once, Alys seemed not to want to look at him directly, lowering her

214

eyes. When, eventually, she did look at him and make her signs, there was no misreading them. *'Belle won't want me there. I know how she feels.'*

Quinlan said, 'You're going there. With me.'

More flickering of hands and fingers and a raising of eyebrows. *'What if she flies into a rage, and leaves?'*

'Belle must do whatever she thinks she has to do. I still want you with me.' Then, blinking his terrible eyes. 'You *want* to come?'

After a moment or two, studying his ravaged face, a slow nodding, then a touch of silken fingers. She had no need of speech.

Quinlan's big arm across her shoulders, they walked slowly away.

THE END

RIDERS OF RIFLE RANGE
Wade Hamilton

Veterinarian Jeff Jones did not like open warfare — but it was there on Scrub Pine grass. When he diagnosed a sick bull on the Endicott ranch as having the contagious blackleg disease, he got involved in the warfare — whether he liked it or not!

BEAR PAW
Nevada Carter

Austin Dailey traded two cows to a pair of Indians for a bay horse, which subsequently disappeared. Tracks led to a secret hideout of fugitive Indians — and cattle thieves. Indians and stockmen co-operated against the rustlers. But it was Pale Woman who acted as interpreter between her people and the rangemen.

THE WEST WITCH
Lance Howard

Detective Quinton Hilcrest journeys west, seeking the Black Hood Bandits' lost fortune. Within hours of arriving in Hags Bend, he is fighting for his life, ensnared with a beautiful outcast the town claims is a witch! Can he save the young woman from the angry mob?

GUNS OF THE PONY EXPRESS
T. M. Dolan

Rich Zennor joined the Pony Express venture at the start, as second-in-command to tough Denning Hartman. But Zennor had the problems of Hartman believing that they had crossed trails in the past, and the fact that he was strongly attached to Hartman's Indian girl, Conchita.